A NOVEL

In the Light of Winter

NANCY HANNAN

Editorial development and creative design support by Ascent:
www.itsyourlifebethere.com

ISBN: 978-1-979-96676-4
Printed in the United States of America

This book is dedicated to the memory of

my beloved Uncle Jack

and

his lovely Kathryn

To Ami,

There is someone

special for everyone —

Keep looking — life will

lead you to each other —

Best wishes —

Nancy

/Samson

6/2/18

ACKNOWLEDGEMENTS

First, I want to thank David Hazard, my writing coach and editor for the third time, for his professional guidance and input. When my guru told me to write a love story for the older age group I decided to try it. David came up with a time frame and suggestions . . . and kept me focused.

I also want to thank Peter Gloege, my book designer, who also did my last two books. I had an idea for the cover of this book but when he and David showed me their version, I was more than delighted.

And I cannot say enough for Denise della Santina, my proof reader. She was a delight to work with. Knowledgeable, well traveled, articulate, and meticulous. Thank you so much, Denise.

Love is eternal, and the search for it, universal, regardless of age. So when I mentioned to some friends and acquaintances that the novel I was writing was a love story for those, late in life who found themselves single again, I was surprised at how many began to share their own experiences with me. Good and bad.

It was interesting to see a common thread running through many of those stories, validating much of what I had already written.

I am most grateful to those of you who not only shared your stories with me, but gave me permission to weave into my novel, the well—disguised snippets from your lives.

The book is not based on any one person or persons. The characters in it are fictitious, composites, and the product of my imagination. Except for Lia, who is based on my long time friend, Lee Moorhead, better known as the Psychic of The Hamptons who now lives in Myrtle Beach, SC.

*If God gave me
one more piece of life...*

*I would take advantage
of that time*

*and prove to men
how wrong they are*

*to think that they stop falling in love
as they get older,*

*since they actually get older
when they stop*

falling in love.

—GABRIEL GARCIA MARQUEZ

P R O L O G U E

"I'M SEEING A TALL, slender woman with red hair...a mother figure." Anne, the medium, spoke softly but deliberately, then asked, "Is your mother on the other side?"

I answered affirmatively.

"Yes, I believe this is your mother," she said. "She's holding a toolbox in one hand and is handing you a screwdriver with the other. There's something she wants you to do with it."

Then that's not my mother, I thought. *The medium is wrong. Mom wouldn't know what to do with a toolbox.*

How many times had I heard her say, "When your father gets home, he'll have to fix it."

The medium opened her eyes and looked at me. "Your mother is smiling. She wants you to know that she does know what to do with a toolbox. She wants me to tell you that they continue to learn on the other side, and she knows what to do with the tools inside the box."

A shock went through me. There was no way the medium could have known my thoughts.

While I was regaining composure, I thought about Father Gavigan, my Jesuit mentor for many years. In our numerous discussions on the metaphysical, or unseen world, he advised me to continue to search and to be open. "There is so much we don't know, just continue to look," he would say, "and you'll find your answers."

He further surprised me by telling me. "Read Edgar Casey."

Casey was considered out-of-bounds for Roman Catholics and other conservative Christians at that time, but at Father Gavigan's suggestion, I read him anyway.

And as I read his books I began to feel quite comfortable with the belief that we do indeed, move on in the next life, sometimes returning for soul growth. We are not stationary beings, worshiping God in quiet contemplation, but we are rather alive, continuing to learn and grow.

I returned from my momentary digression to find Anne patiently waiting.

I didn't visit her often, but had studied under her some years ago, and found her to be accurate and reliable both in her psychic readings and as a medium.

My first husband, the children's father, had died several years before, and although I'd been in two caring relationships after his death, I did not remarry until a couple of years ago. That second marriage was a disaster and had just ended. I felt a need for some direction and advice, which is why I had come to see Anne.

When I smiled and nodded, she went on.

"Your mother wants you to go to *a certain room* and take the door off," she said. "Not unlock it, *take it off.* Do you know what she's talking about?"

I slowly nodded my head yes. My mother must have been referring to a poem I had written long before, but had never shown her. . .*how did she know about it?*

THE SECRET ROOM

*So many times have I been asked
To share the treasure locked away.
As many times I would refuse
For no one had the key.*

*In thought, I'd peek inside the room
To find my treasure still intact.
The passion I kept locked away
Is saved for him who has the key.*

Anne continued: "Your mother feels that your heart is locked in that room and you are waiting for the right person to find the key to unlock the door. But that won't happen. She wants you to take the door *off,* free your heart and search for him yourself. *You must open your heart,* she's telling me. You have kept it locked away far too long.

You know what you're looking for. You must *search for him yourself.*"

I found it strange that my mother would be so open and understanding in such matters. When I was growing up I rarely felt comfortable talking to her about anything personal. In fact, I kept such things to myself, probably out of fear of criticism or ridicule. Back then, we were not encouraged to think outside of the box as everything was either black or white. As a child and even as a teen, I was overly sensitive to negative judgment. It was much easier to hide my thoughts and feelings.

Now, she was encouraging me to be open and free. Where was this encouragement when I needed it earlier in my life?

Again, as if she knew my private thoughts, Anne added, "She wants you to know they are *all very happy for you now.* They were not happy when you married your second husband, and they're glad he is out of your life." Anne paused as though to assimilate another thought. "Are you building a house? Your mother says that she's glad your house is almost finished."

"No," I told her, "just making some repairs on the one I own, and replacing what needs to be replaced."

She's telling me that you have begun to reclaim your life, and that's good. Now it's time for you to move on. Be open. Be who you need to be. Build a new life. And to do it, you're going to need new 'tools.' Do you understand?"

I nodded that I did.

As I drove away, I thought to myself, *Why did I say yes when I'm not even sure how to build a new life—and I haven't done very well creating a new relationship so far. . . .*

If I was going to move on from here, find happiness, and God help me, open myself to love again, I would need new skills. "Tools" was a good word, I suppose. But how would I learn to be more skilled in the art of relationships this late in life, I wondered?

Those questions faded into the background as I drove home, overtaken by the realization that we are not forgotten by those close to us who have passed over. That thought was more than comforting. In fact, even more than remembering us, they appear to watch over us as well. And the fact that we continue to learn on the other side is uplifting. How can we possibly learn all there is to learn in one lifetime? Their presence and guidance made sense to me. Those who can see from a higher level are able to see what we cannot.

Would they continue to help me now, facing life alone, once more? I certainly hoped so.

And then a final thought settled in: I was far from ready to search for anyone, and maybe never would be. At the moment, it felt too good to be free again. I liked my life the way it was now!

(That would not last for long.)

CHAPTER ONE

Alone

"KATE, WE BOTH KNOW there's no socially acceptable way to grieve after a divorce, but you can't stay in hiding forever." Nora had been my rock during the divorce, and having been there / done that, she understood my reluctance to mingle so soon after. But that didn't stop her from slowly dragging me back into the real world.

I just wasn't ready; it's a solitary path back into the real world, and I needed time to adjust and to think, so I buried myself in a series of necessary and time-consuming activities, among them, returning to the work force.

Uncomfortable with my new label—"divorced"—I preferred to work where I would not be surrounded by men, so I decided I to look for a teaching position.

After all, I had a master's degree in English. . .and my substituting over the years at the local community college would have some leverage. I hoped so anyway, because there was an opening at a nearby private college and my credentials were up to date.

At home, my duties were cut out for me while I struggled to put my house in good order. Some rooms needed fresh paint, the leaking shower needed a plumber, the burned out ceiling lights in the garage needed replacing. The stained carpets in two rooms needed to be replaced as well. Working part time, I would carefully divide my lists of "things to do" into a workable schedule. Then there was church and the activities provided there.

Still, there was time left over—but after this last marriage, I had no desire to meet a new man right now. So I told myself over and over.

That did not stop some of my friends from urging me to jump right back into the mating pool. The ever-watchful Nora would see to it that I didn't. But she couldn't be everywhere.

"Come here and look at this, Kate," my doctor's wife (and assistant) said to me one day as I came out of her husband's office. She had pulled up some photos on her computer: I found myself looking at several available men on Senior Match.com.

"This one's adorable, look at his crop of wavy grey hair and he has a great profile!" She flashed a few more tempting visions in front of me.

"Sorry, Kelly, I really am not ready to go that route. . .not now, anyway." But she had planted a seed. When I was ready, I might try online dating. . .even though it did not feel right to me.

Another friend did not even ask. She put me on Match.com using a rather good photo of me she had in her possession. At first I was mortified. Then. . .okay. . .the profile was so complimentary I just couldn't delete it.

No, no, no, I thought, *you're not ready.*

But on cool evenings I wished for the feel of warm arms around me. And when I was unsure about a house repair I found myself wanting someone close, to talk out a problem I didn't know how to resolve, to bolster my confidence I was making right choices and spending money wisely. I appreciated a male's viewpoint. . .especially if he was a friend.

In the end I deleted some of the hyperbole from the profile, and watered it down.

Two days later, Nora stopped by with a scolding look. "Kate, your house is not going to be on the local house tour, so take a break. Next thing I know you'll be wallpapering the garage. Are you coming out with us Friday eveningor not?"

"I'll be getting ready for painters to come in this weekend, so. . .how about a rain check?"

"We gave you rain checks the last four times we asked you out and you turned us down. You're on your own, girlfriend."

And so, my friends backed off from inviting me anywhere because I was "too busy" to go places or do things with them. Secretly, I felt that getting out of my own head was the very thing I needed. Instead, I created busy work, enrolled in college courses, and remained obsessed with returning my home to the clean, orderly haven it had once been.

Take the door off the room. . .you have tools in your tool bag. Use them. . . .

The words I'd heard from the last meeting with Anne had stuck with me. I just didn't know exactly how to move ahead with what they were telling me to do. And maybe I didn't want the door taken off the room just yet. Maybe I wasn't ready to let someone new tamper with my heart. I busied myself in the busyness of fixing up my outer world.

First, I tossed out anything soiled beyond repair, painted dirty rooms, and replaced furniture, carpets, and curtains. The place needed to be mine again: my own favorite scent—lavender, vanilla—placement of antiques and *objets d'art*, music that elicited joy and relaxation, aroma of foods that whetted my appetite. My now former husband had barked that placing seed in the bird feeders would "attract rats." I love the birds and their song; I loaded several new feeders around the house with seed.

Little by little, the house took on a persona of its' own. It had been a happy, fun place, a home base for the family, and a meeting place for friends. . . .before Alan. I blamed myself for making this choice. He had been so kind and solicitous before we married. Maybe there was something in me I needed to look at. . . .

For now, I was only determined to return the house to a condition that felt right to me.

My dream had always been to share this house and my gardens—my little piece of the planet—with someone special in my later years, once the children were on their own. Now they were. And here I was. . .alone.

Maybe, I thought, *I should just deal with reality. Maybe I'll never get to realize that dream of a second true love. Not everyone does.*

And underneath it all I was just not ready, and doubted if I ever would be, to enter into another relationship.

I could not help my mind from drifting back to the most recent disaster. . . .

After the youngest child had left home I'd felt I was ready for a companion. Their father was long deceased, and I wanted a partner, someone with whom to share my life, and so I remarried.

Alan and I met on common ground and had mutual friends, but I found out too late that we did not really know each other at all. He was a nice guy, attentive, religious, and he actively pursued me. We had a lovely wedding, but within months, I realized I'd made a big mistake.

The caring and respect I'd hoped for after my first marriage was drowned in an ocean of indifference and disinterest in anything I loved or liked.

Loneliness can be a dangerous drug leading to bad decisions. . .like Alan. At least, the divorce was a mutual decision, but my beautiful haven was a wreck from two years of neglect.

After I tackled most of the projects involving the house itself, I took on the lawn and gardens. Bare patches in the lawn were rehabilitated—bare spots that reminded me how Alan had shown little interest in keeping a lovely environment—and new rosebushes and perennial beds surrounded the house.

With each bit of ground regained I felt a surge of triumph. Yes, the place was once more fully mine.

Now all I need is to find the love of my life to share this with.

Ugh. That thought again. I'd tried to find that before, and it had not worked out.

A new thought crossed my mind. *Maybe you should take some responsibility for the choice you made. After all. . .*

I stopped that thought from developing. After all, *what?*

Was I supposed to blame myself for marrying a man who probably didn't really love me?

(He validated that thought by remarrying less than a year later.)

No. I didn't need to blame myself. Of that I was sure. After Alan was out the door, I searched my soul and psyche, read anything that could help make sense of the past couple years and even sought professional help.

No, I'd dug around my soul enough. Now I just needed to keep the ghosts and memories of the past in the past.

Yes, that was it. Perhaps Alan had served a purpose—he certainly made me wiser about love—and after our ill- fated marriage, I worked hard to chalk the experience up to life lessons learned and continued to pray for a companion, a partner, someone I-hopefully-could love, and who would love me back.

All that remained for me was to make peace with myself and my situation. After all, I was older. Who would want me now?

As I sat alone on my newly cleaned deck, or on the screened porch, or the bench out back on the secluded patio, I gazed at sunset after sunset and the stars that followed them. Evening after evening, I listened to the sounds of summer nights—the crickets and the night birds there had become my only company.

What I needed was to find a way to live with an emptiness that begged to be filled. Everything about my home was now as I wanted it. I was surrounded by lovely gardens, a perfect lawn and. . .

. . .insufferable loneliness.

My chest sometimes ached with it. I wanted so badly for someone new to enter my space.

But had I healed sufficiently, or searched deeply enough to know what I wanted?

Open your heart.

All right Kate, I whispered to myself one late summer evening. *Let's do this. Let's see what happens.*

Late into the night I allowed myself to look at the unbelievable mass of possibilities on Match.com.

Thank you, girlfriend, for setting me up, I thought, shaking my head.

I only hope I don't want to kill you later!

Every day, computer-generated "perfect matches" filled my inbox wasting valuable time as I carefully scrutinized each one. After a while, I was able to delete without even reading the profile. Weeks into the new experience, I had yet to reply to any of them, fearful he might reply in return. *Then,* what would I do?!

I realize times are different now, and I am older, but I'm not sure about this new way of moving from the singles scene into the couples' scene. I *do* want a partner, a companion, someone I can love again. . .and *I want my space, too.*

Still, I prefer to meet someone the old fashioned way, like I did the year after my first husband died. I did not choose him from an online list, it just happened.

CHAPTER TWO

The Old-Fashioned Way

I COULDN'T IMAGINE who would be sending me a wedding invitation. I didn't recognize the handwriting so I opened the envelope carefully.

Why did I have to be reminded about love and marriage now, with Ed so recently gone?

Louise, the daughter of good friends from our old neighborhood, was getting married. Even though we'd kept in touch since they moved, I had not seen them for some time. It would be great to see the whole family again.

But I wasn't sure how comfortable I would be going

alone to a formal wedding with the reception at the elegant Pierre in New York City. The single life is too new for me to feel comfortable at such an affair, let alone, one at *that* location.

What an unfortunate coincidence. . .Ed and I had stayed at the Pierre Hotel near Central Park on our honeymoon.

Although it had been a year, how would I feel being there this soon after his passing? Would I remember that happy day or would it remind me that the love of my life was now gone?

After much thought, I felt it was best for me to decline the invitation. I'd just send them a nice gift.

But the family would not accept my decision. After weeks of back and forth phone calls from the bride's mother, and a pleading call from the bride's sister, I agreed to go.

"We just want you to be there. It doesn't matter if you are alone."

Easy for them to say. I knew I would have to face the world as a single woman one day, but I wasn't ready to do it right now. . .it's not that easy to change pace after being married for so long. And then to suddenly become a widow at sixty-five. . . . But I promised them I would go. I could always make an appearance and then slip out unnoticed, early.

The sun was shining and I detected a light breeze on that very warm, humid August morning as I put my overnight bag in the trunk of the car. I braced myself for the drive into the Big Apple—another first and hopefully, not too big a challenge on my road to independence.

This being on my own thing could be unnerving at times, especially when the unpredictable suddenly reared its head. A road trip opened up ample possibilities for surprises to occur, and not all necessarily the good kind.

Fortunately, I had a good map and clear directions to both the church and the reception.

My concerns about traveling on my own were unfounded, and in less time than I expected, I was in Manhattan with no problem at all. I found the cathedral with a minimum of effort and was able to park less than a block away, so had time to spare. I crossed the street to get a better view of the tall, old church, which was a historic landmark in the city.

As I re-crossed the street and headed toward the cathedral, I heard my name called. I turned to see a familiar couple, Carmen and Maria, the bride's aunt and uncle, trying to catch up with me. I had not seen them since their relatives moved back to New York.

We always looked forward to their visits to Virginia. Not only because they were fun, but because they would bring wonderful Italian delicacies such as sausages, salumi, mortadella, parmesan cheese from Parma, and a cache of desserts I'd never heard of. Seeing them again was like old times, and I felt myself relax a little about being here on my own.

After big welcoming hugs—it was obvious that we still had a warm connection—they both talked at the same time, as I tried to distinguish who was saying what. I'd forgotten they talked like this, over the top of one another, but it all came back to me, and I laughed.

"We're so happy you came up," Maria said. "Mary Sue told us you were coming." The bride's mother was southern and used a double name, which the Italians thought strange. Mary Sue thought some of the Italians' habits were strange, too. It was funny, knowing both viewpoints, which each concealed from the other. Yes, I was right back in the thick of it, at least with these wonderful old friends.

"You're sitting with us," Maria said, as Carmen concurred, bobbing his head up and down.

"But you will be sitting with the family," I responded.

She cut me short. "You have always been family Kate. You're sitting with us." And so my hesitance was overruled.

Inside the cathedral, the three of us sat in the second row right behind the family matriarch, who seemed as happy to see me as I was to see her. At one point during the Mass, she turned around and whispered, "Kate, when should I go up to communion?" This was a detail someone had obviously forgotten to tell her. I smiled and told her when it would be time for her to follow everyone else up to the altar rail.

Then and there I knew I'd done the right thing by coming. After a time of such deep loss and retreating into myself, life was beginning to feel good again.

This was a typical Italian Catholic wedding—well planned, down to the tiniest detail. I could only imagine what the reception would be like.

The Pierre was a short distance from the cathedral, and when the elevator opened into the spacious reception area, I was greeted by the loveliest sight. Tall vases of orchids mixed with elegant summer flowers anchored each large, round, white-draped table, transforming the room into an island paradise. Stunning.

I felt a twinge of. . .too many feelings at once. Nostalgia. Joy. Sadness. Grief. Once again, for a moment, I wondered if this had really been a good idea. *Maybe I should have driven home instead of coming here.*

Searching for my name among the sea of place settings, I finally found the one with my name on it. Unfortunately, I didn't recognize anyone at the table, but before I could pull my chair out, the gentleman to my right got up and did it for me.

"Hi, I'm Nick," he said, with a cheerful look as I sat down.

I extended my hand and smiled back at him. "Kate Murphy."

The woman I took to be his wife was animatedly talking to the couple on her right, and just as I was seated, the waiter came to take our drink order. Turning to me, Nick asked, "What would you like?"

"It's probably too early for a martini," I hesitated, "but I'll have one anyway."

"It's one o'clock!" he laughed, "that's not too early!" Then he looked up at the waiter, "two martinis, no vermouth, two olives."

Then quickly turning to me, "I'm sorry, I should have asked if you wanted vermouth and an olive." I couldn't help but smile. "As it happens, that's exactly the way I like it." I liked his take-charge attitude, but it was something else that made me smile. That old comfortable feeling of someone ordering what I liked—as if he knew.

By the time the waiter returned with our table's drinks, the music was playing.

"Would you like to dance?" Nick asked, breaking off our small-talk conversation. I hesitated. "But we just got our drinks. Do you want to dance, *now*?"

"Sure. Now. If your drink gets warm, I'll get you another one."

The woman next to him was still holding forth in conversation, so I got up and headed out onto the gleaming parquet dance floor with him.

Nick was a good dancer, a nice looking man, graying at the temples, obviously older than I, and he seemed like a fun person.

The sumptuous feast lasted for hours, while the music was constant—fortunately, much of it danceable for an older age group. The second time Nick asked me to dance, I felt a bit uncomfortable, but his wife was still so involved in conversation with the other couple—obviously they had a lot to catch up on—it did not seem to bother either of them that he and I were dancing.

Maybe she doesn't like to dance, I thought.

After the third dance, I stopped to thank her for allowing her husband to dance with the single gal at the table.

"Oh," she said with a laugh, "Nick's not my husband. This is the cousins' table and the family has been trying to fix the two of us up ever since he lost his wife. He's at this table because of me, but they don't know we're not interested in each other. He is the business partner of the bride's father. He's a great guy," she broke off to address Nick, "Nick you're a great guy!" Then back to me, "But he's all yours!"

When I got back to my place I looked at Nick for a moment.

"Why didn't you tell me?"

He shrugged his shoulders, "You didn't ask!"

And before I had time to sit down he took my hand and led me back to the dance floor. Halfway through the dance, he danced me over to the family area, saying, "Let's go see what the newlyweds are doing."

I spotted my old friends, Maria and Carmen and as we

got closer to their table, they rose to greet us.

I don't know which happened first, them getting up to greet us, or Nick's comment, "I'd like you to meet my brother and his wife," but it was a strange and wonderful moment.

I'd been having a ball with the *brother* of my old friend. . .a man who was also the business partner of the bride's father.

You can imagine the conversation that followed. We stood by their table while the bride cut the cake, and very shortly, we were all clapping as shy little Louise endured the Italian custom of being carried aloft in a chair while being paraded around the room to joyful music.

As Nick and I walked back to our table, for a brief moment, I experienced that oh so comfortable feeling of being part of an extended family again. Connected and not alone.

A little while later, the festivities started to wind down and a few guests were saying their good-byes.

Nick turned to me. "It's too early to leave. By the way, where are *you* staying?"

"I'm planning to head back to Virginia this evening," I told him.

He would have none of it. "What? It's too late to drive that far. Other guests are staying at my place, and I have plenty of room. You should spend the night, too, and drive home in the morning."

I staved off giving him an answer long enough to check with his business partner, my long-time friend, and father of the bride.

"Do take him up on the offer," he reassured me, "you'll be perfectly safe. He's a wonderful guy, very proper, with a lovely home. You'll be fine. Please, do not drive back to Virginia tonight, Kate."

Nick was *indeed* a perfect gentleman. The other guests retired early but he and I stayed up talking well into the early hours.

"I hope we can see each other again sometime," he said with a questioning look on his face.

"I rarely get up this way," I told him, "except to visit my daughter, who lives in Boston, and I have a sister in White

Plains, though I don't visit her too often."

"Well, the next time you go to see either of them, why not divert your plans and stop off here on the way. I'll pick you up at LaGuardia, we can have dinner, and then you can catch the next flight to Boston or White Plains."

I would think about it, I told him, doubting seriously that he and I would ever see each other after this evening. It was too far away and I had a house to sell in the aftermath of my husband's death.

Exhaustion finally caught up with me. "I think it's bedtime and I'm really tired," I told him, "it's been a wonderful day and I have a long drive tomorrow. But thank you so much for letting me stay here tonight, I'll be forever grateful."

He apologized for keeping me up so late and walked me to the guest room down the hall from his. "That's the bathroom," he said, pointing. He kissed my hand lightly, told me to "sleep tight," and went to his room.

I closed the door to my room, slipped out of my silk dress and crawled into bed.

Nice as the day had been, nice as he was, I was not going to involve myself with this man.

When I got out of the shower the next morning, with a fresh toothbrush and towel laid out and a dab of makeup from my purse, I smelled bacon frying and fresh coffee brewing. I imagined I had spent the night at the Pierre.

"Where's the other couple?" I asked as I noticed only two places set on the breakfast table. He told me they had gone to bed so early the night before because they had to leave by six, so it was just the two of us.

We thoroughly enjoyed our leisurely breakfast. The conversation was animated and interesting and I would have enjoyed staying, but had a six-hour drive ahead of me and wanted to get going. Nick gave me excellent directions for getting out of New York along with an open invitation—"You can visit anytime."

When he opened the car door for me, he stood in front of it. Planting a gentle kiss on my cheek, he gave me a hug. "Don't lose my phone number," he said, and closed my car door.

Driving along the Hudson River, I thought how beautiful everything looked. *The air smelled so clean, the flowers looked brighter, the sky seemed bluer, everything seemed. . .prettier.*

Back home, I needed to take stock of my life. Where was I going? While I cherished the peace and freedom of widowhood, I hated being alone. *Can one have a life of her own and love,* I wondered?

I had no idea I would be facing that dilemma so soon.

Two weeks later, I found myself writing a short letter—trying to stay noncommittal.

August 20

"Dear Nick,

It was nice hearing from you the other day. Glad you received my 'thank you" note. Yes, in answer to your question, I am planning to visit my daughter in Boston for her birthday in two weeks. If you are still interested in my stopping off to have dinner with you, I can take the 4:30 shuttle arriving at LaGuardia at 5:30. Let me know. We can eat somewhere near the airport, if that suits you, and I can catch the last shuttle to Boston at 9:30.

Take care, Kate

August 23

Dear Kate,

I will be at the shuttle terminal by 5:15. There is a decent restaurant not too far from the airport. And the last shuttle leaves at 10:30. Looking forward to seeing you.

My Best, Nick

As I deplaned at LaGuardia, I saw someone holding a huge sign with my name on it. Surely, it couldn't be *him,* but it was.

"Please put that sign down," I whispered, a bit embarrassed.

We got into his Mercedes and I commentated on how nice it smelled. "It's baby powder," Nick said. "I was told you don't like the smell of cigars so I sprayed the car. Hope you can't smell the cigar."

Hm. So he'd done his homework about me.

The evening turned out fine. We chatted a bit, relived the wedding and dinner was nice. We didn't have to rush to make the 9:30 shuttle—I stuck to my original plan—and fortunately, my daughter worked late so did not mind picking me up at 10:30.

A week or two later, he called to see if I could come up that Friday. He had tickets to a local theatre and would like me to go with him. Uneasy about the sleeping arrangements—he wanted me to stay at his place again, and this time I would be alone with him—I declined, but didn't tell him why.

The following week, my sister in White Plains invited me up for a visit. This I could handle. Another stopover, have dinner with him, and continue on the short flight to Marge's small, local airport.

When Nick picked me up, we didn't go to the nearby airport restaurant. "I'm taking you to a nice place tonight," he said as we drove away. "It's in Garden City, near home. I'd like you to stay overnight so we can have a leisurely

dinner and an opportunity to talk. . .why not call your sister and tell her you changed your plans and will be there
tomorrow?"

I called Marge, as he suggested, and stayed overnight.

The next week he called again.

I was not sure what I was doing at this point. It had
been more than 25 years since I'd dated. I felt off-balance.
I wished I'd spent more time with my own heart to know
how I was feeling about all this, but the truth was I had so
many tender and lonely feelings I tried to keep myself busy
and *not* feel too much.

Nick was very up front—again, something I liked.

"There's an engagement party next month and I want
to make sure you're available," he said. "My cousin is getting married and I want you to meet his family."

At his insistence I checked my calendar, which was
blank. "I think I might be available," I informed him.

To further entice me, he continued, "Carmen and
Maria will be there, and we don't want to disappoint them.
Just bring a nice dress for the party and something casual

for the other two days."

I paused. Did I really want to do this? Wasn't this moving too fast? On the other hand, how long were you supposed to wait at this age for "the right one" to come along? Nick was a great guy. . .pleasant and considerate. . . .

Sensing my reluctance to spend a whole weekend, he added, "You can still stay in the guest room, like before."

"Well. . ."

"Look Kate, I'm not a bashful guy. Maybe you've noticed. So I'm gonna go for it. The party is a month away and I really want to see you."

My reluctance was eroding.

"So how about this weekend? No plans, no hurry to catch a plane back, just some nice quiet time. A drive up the Hudson maybe, or some local shopping, leisurely dinner Saturday and the shuttle back after lunch Sunday."

The thought of kind companionship did it. And I did want to get to know him better.

I flew up that Friday. "Not eating out tonight," he informed me. "I want you to sample my homemade meatballs and spaghetti sauce." Meatballs were apparently his specialty. . .the freezer was full of them.

Again, I slept in the guest room. The next morning he fried bacon, put the coffee on and scrambled the eggs. . .but did allow me to butter the toast.

We drove up the parkway along the Hudson, enjoyed the breathtakingly beautiful scenery and made light conversation. It was a delightful day. That evening we dined at Portofino. In time, it would become one of our favorite places to eat: You could cut the "vee la" chop with a fork it was so tender.

Sunday, Nick reluctantly went to Mass with me. It was the first time he had been in a Catholic church since his wife had died two years before. We visited one of his in-laws for lunch then off to LaGuardia and back to Virginia.

I had survived the weekend without any challenges I couldn't handle and without any remorse.

Thus began my love affair with airports and the shuttle. I would fly to New York on Fridays, and return home on Sunday. On Friday I would toss my suitcase on the guest room bed where it stayed until Sunday morning.

In short order I was accompanying him to every family baptism, first communion, confirmation, ball game, engagement party, wedding, funeral and any other occasion that called for the usual Italian gastronomic fare of sausages, lasagna, pasta, cannelloni, pies, and on and on. The only things that differentiated any function were the clothes. . .otherwise, same people, same food, same conversation. This Italian family not only celebrated *everything*, but anyone remotely related came out of the woodwork for the occasion.

It was fun. Sheer fun. And how could I feel alone in a laughing, bantering crowd like this? This was what I'd wanted, wasn't it, to feel connected?

Very quickly Nick drew me into his social circle, as well.

He was active in the Lions Club, a group that took their objectives seriously. I came to know the other ladies who were quite friendly and I soon looked forward to the social activities, which were always held at very nice restaurants. Once in a while, they had a dinner-dance at a hotel.

I soon became close to his extended family, especially his sister-in-law and her husband. They took me under their wing and attempted to integrate Irish me into Italian them. And a transition from being single to being part of a couple again, with an extended family felt like just the magic I needed.

One weekend, Carmen and Maria asked us to drive out to the Hamptons with them to check out a new, gated community in Southampton. They had been looking for a place near the water for some time, and this condo was within their means.

An expert in real estate, Nick would be a great help to his brother.

After hours of comparison and discussion, they narrowed the possibilities down to three units.

There was one unit I felt had more potential than the other two. "It has a lovely view of the water from the upstairs bedroom," I interjected, "and no one can build in front of it blocking the view of the ocean," I added.

"You're right. . .hadn't thought of that," Carmen said, "just not sure though."

As for me, I had never been out to the Hamptons before, and found the area delightful. Hopefully, I would get to visit them from time to time after they purchased a home there.

The next time Nick called, I asked him which condo his brother bought. "None of them," he said, "but *I* bought the one you liked."

I couldn't believe it. What would he do with another house? He'll probably hire a decorator as he had for his city home, but who would take care of it?

It wasn't long before he asked me if I would furnish and decorate it. He gave me an ample budget, and I was able to do both. . .down to the last fork.

Nick made it clear. "This is mainly my summer home, but you have the use of it anytime you want."

I stayed in Southampton more than Virginia that year.

Two years later, Nick showed me his will, in which he left the house in Southampton to me.

I was overwhelmed. We had never discussed the future, just made casual references to it.

As time went by, Nick and I were simply living life as it propelled us, day by day. And although busy with their own lives, my kids visited from time to time."You look happy, Mom." That was all that mattered to them.

But, as time went by, I slowly realized that all was *not* well. Little by little, I had begun to back away from this fairy tale life. The house in Virginia, still unsold, gave me some grief and I needed to make decisions. But that was not the real reason I found myself backing up.

For all the good times we had together, something vital was missing from the relationship, and I was not sure what it was.

True, Nick was easy to be with, rarely complained, criticized, or disagreed with me. Whatever I did was fine. I was not used to that. There was never any discussion about what I bought for the house, either. If I suggested purchasing something, his answer was always, "Whatever you think. . .or want."

But there was also a sense that we were not connected at some deep level. Not really.

Once, concerned about how I looked for a special occasion, I asked Nick if he liked what I was wearing. "You never say anything about how I look," I prompted.

"Because I always like how you look," he answered.

Still, I wondered, did he ever have an opinion about me? Was I always pleasing to him?

In time I began to sense something else. There was no challenge in this relationship. Not that I wanted a struggle, but I did need interaction. We were always so busy meeting the social obligations of family and civic organizations that we did not have time to be *us*.

That was it. We appeared to be a couple, but we were not a unit.

I found my desire for oneness was only partially satisfied. Physical union was not sufficient, though. I needed a union of the spiritual and mind as well. In a healthy relationship there must also be the willingness to confront one another at times, and *there needs to be dialogue*. He and I never had discussions about anything. If we were not going someplace, I read, and he watched TV. We were like two older people finally comfortable after years of living together. . .only we had never done those things that people do together in a marriage.

One day I found myself thinking, *there needs to be passion. Love cannot grow without passion*. And that was missing. One can exist for a time in a comfort zone, but I wanted to live, not exist. I had a passion for life, and wanted to share that passion with someone. I felt he had already lived and was now content to simply exist as long as he was comfortable.

It did not seem fair to prolong this state of indecision, but I was at a loss as to how to extricate myself without hurting him. I needed help.

CHAPTER THREE

The Psychic of The Hamptons

MY FIRST THOUGHT was to contact Anne, the medium, but realized I couldn't wait until I returned to Virginia, I needed help now. But there was a psychic in the area.

I had seen her name in the local paper and had always enjoyed reading her weekly column, but I wasn't sure if she was legitimate. A chance encounter in the local bookstore dispelled any doubts.

"I would never make an important decision without consulting Lia first," I overheard a woman tell her friend. "She's a great psychic, but it's her knowledge of astrology that I depend on."

I was pretending to be reading something so I could hear more, but it finally got the best of me. "I'm, sorry, but I overheard your comments about Lia. Is she really that good?"

"The best! And I've been to them all. Give her a call, she'll be glad to talk to you."

Two days later, I visited Lia at her home. It was a modest, but lovely small cottage, conveniently located in the center of town. As she opened the door, I was immediately impressed by the stately woman with a welcoming, no nonsense, presence, and felt comfortable at once.

"Please, have a seat," she said, pointing to a comfortable chair near her desk, while adjusting her tape recorder.

I looked around the nicely decorated parlor where we would be having the reading. No candles lighting up a darkened room, no ethereal music in the background, no incense burning, nothing to indicate you were off on another planet. Just a normal, cheerful, knowledgeable. . . psychic. . .using her gift to guide anyone who came to her for help.

Nor did she did use generic words that could fit anyone who had the imagination to twist them into what they wanted to hear. She was specific and accurate.

"Relax, Kate, and get comfortable, I've been waiting for you since you called." She readied the tape, and pulled out her deck of Tarot cards.

"Wow, stuff going on around you. . .lots of it," she said.

Then: "You're seriously thinking of leaving that man in your life, aren't you? He's not your husband. I see you with your back to him."

Well then, we were into it. I relayed my feelings and concerns to her. "I just don't know if leaving him is the right thing to do. I hate to hurt him and I don't think he has any idea how I feel. He seems quite content with life as it is, but I'm not."

"Of course he's content," she said. "Why wouldn't he be? You have a beautiful life together. That's coming through clearly. But it's only beautiful on the surface."

So true.

"But you have to be true to yourself, Kate, honor your instincts, your intuition. You haven't always done that, and you need to now. You know it's over, and you do have to tell him, but wait until after summer."

I'm sure I looked perplexed—and probably a bit sad, as well.

"The relationship was not meant to last," she continued. "That's why you never discussed marriage or the future. It has served its purpose and it's time for you to move on. At least you found that you can still feel, and that you're attractive to a man, and can function. That's what you needed to know."

"I also see a house that you're concerned about; it will sell within a few months and you will buy a smaller one a bit further out. . .looks like in horse country. Do you ride?"

She's nuts, I thought. . .*horse country!* I could never afford to live in horse country outside of Washington, DC, where the prices are astronomical. Not in a thousand years.

I looked at her without any recognition of her words— she seemed to pick up the fact that I questioned her comment.

"Well, *I see horses and fences.* And I do see another man coming into your life, someone from the past. He was once in love with you," she added.

Then he must be dead, I thought, and immediately put that out of my mind as well. This was not a time to be sarcastic.

I left with a mixed reaction that day. Some of what she'd said was uncannily accurate. But—horse country? And someone from my past? Highly unlikely.

The rest of the summer was pleasant even with the cloud over my head. Nick and I ate at the usual spots, sat on the beach, visited with family in spurts, and took occasional walks. I attempted to have deeper conversations—and connections—but found there were no topics of mutual interest to engage in. It was sad, but at least I knew for sure what I had to do.

After Labor Day, I packed for the trip back to Virginia with a melancholy in one part of my heart, but surprised at how free the other part felt.

Back home, my work would be cut out for me, and as painful as it would be, I knew I must sell the house. It was more than I needed, costly to maintain, and more time consuming than I needed it to be. That, plus searching for another home would take up my time, energy and thought— and that helped to dispel any sadness I was carrying inside at the thought of ending it with Nick.

"I'll be down to see you soon," he said, after kissing me good-bye that last day of summer. I drove away with true regret in my heart, still not knowing how or when I would tell him.

It was a lovely fall day when I picked him up at National

Airport. That evening we sat in the too-large living room of my home before going out to dinner. I made each of us a martini, no vermouth, two olives.

And told him.

He said he saw it coming but found it hard to accept.

I hugged him as a mother would a child, and gave no other reason than when one phase of life is over, it's because another is waiting for us somewhere.

But he was not the only sad person in the room. I was too. . .maybe sadder, as I envisioned strangers sitting in this lovely bright room, calling the house my husband and I had built to live in forever, *home*. In addition, I was leaving the only man in my life.

Someone once said that sadness precedes joy. I hoped whoever said it was right.

CHAPTER FOUR

New House

THE HOME ED AND I BUILT during our marriage sold, just as Lia said it would, and since I had a few months before settlement, I concentrated on finding a new one. But it wasn't easy. In my price range, I was forced to change my mindset and accept the sorry fact that I would never find a smaller version of the quality home I had been used to.

"Do not show me a split level or wall to wall carpeting," I told my realtor as I continued to follow her around, rejecting every house she showed me.

My intensity about this shocked me. But then, I would defer to Ed when we built our home and was not always allowed to choose exactly what I'd wanted in a home. Now that I was on my own, this was my chance to get what *I* wanted.

"I'd like you to as least look at this one," she said over the phone that morning. "It's a bit further out than you want, but it does have a garage and lots of trees. . .and. . .possibilities." That dreaded word, *possibilities.*

"OK, I'll look—but *just* look."

The rooms were too small. I hated the paint colors; it had wall-to-wall carpet, ugly orange wallpaper in the hallway, the hardware was cheap, the doors were inexpensive builder quality, the bathrooms had to go, as did the vent in the family room ceiling for the wood burning stove they had removed, and it was halfway to nowhere.

But it was the rusted, half-broken chain link fence around the back yard that really set me off. It was terrible.

Then, as I stood in the small foyer, I noticed something. If I looked straight ahead through the triple picture window, I had a clear view of the back yard. I paused, almost walked out the front door—then let myself be drawn to the back of the house. Maybe just a peek.

Out behind the house, tall oak trees overshadowed the scattered pines in the wooded area to the left. The lawn sloped down a bit at that point and I envisioned azaleas at the edge of the lawn where it met the woods.

Something was speaking to me. Not so much the house itself—God knew—but the magical, private setting.

The long driveway was lined with more pine trees, creating a majestic arch. To further enhance the beauty of the property, it was bordered with twenty-one additional pines.

From deep inside, I had a feeling.

Here, I could have utter privacy, and experience nature at its best. Why was I so concerned about the mess inside, when I had sufficient funds from the sale of the old house to update the interior of this one?

I might have recognized then what was going on inside me: the draw to beauty and solitude. And the excitement

I was feeling about creating a whole environment exactly to my own liking.

I was able to obtain an affordable mortgage and purchased the house. I then began the slow process of upgrading and transforming the unacceptable into the acceptable.

It was a far cry from the lovely home my husband and I had built in McLean, but this one was mine. Truly, the nice thing about making all of these decisions was that I didn't have to consider anyone else's taste or ask their permission, although I did discuss changes with my daughter who was away at college in another state.

Slowly, that winter, the house began to take on a shape of its own and I thought there was a good chance I would come to feel comfortable in it. I crossed my fingers and hoped so.

During the weekdays I was fully occupied meeting with and directing the work of the contractors—a deeply satisfying feeling.

Sometimes when the work became too much I had to force myself not to look back, and gradually, my efforts paid off. It was not long before the house smelled, looked and felt like my home. And by the spring, I had come to love my tiny, isolated piece of the planet.

Having focused all my energies on renovating the inside to this point, it was now time to tackle the yard and gardens. And with the beautiful renewal of spring, another feeling made itself known.

Weekdays were full, but then came the weekends. That was when it hit me most: You can only run so many errands, and only do so much yard work and gardening, and you can only enjoy your own company and think your own thoughts so much. Friday and Saturday evenings, I felt the effects of being, not just on my own, but *alone*.

So, while I enjoyed my privacy—mostly—the problem was that my new home was not on the way to anywhere. Old friends no longer just dropped by as I'd been used to them doing. Now, they would call first or wait to be invited. I was simply too far out for casual drop-ins.

It's funny how much you learn about yourself in isolation. In a lot of company I sometimes felt overwhelmed, and craved some space and alone time. Alone and isolated, I learned some part of me was also very much a social being. A new balance would have to be struck.

And so, in addition to seeing my friends more, the matter of dating arose again.

Since the break up with Nick, I'd been happy taking a break from relationships. Now, having thrown my energy almost totally into purchasing and refurbishing a new property, I felt that maybe. . .maybe. . .I was ready to try again.

How would I meet anyone, though, in this country location? *Maybe at church,* I thought. I would have to find a new church, anyway, since my old church was now too far away.

Once again, I found myself dreaming about finding someone special. Someone maybe to share this lovely home with me. Was such a person out there? Or would I find that I needed my space? Could I have both my space and love? I didn't know, but wanted to find out.

At least the new church I planned to attend was conveniently nearby, and soon after I registered for membership, they had an open house for new parishioners. Quite a few parishioners—both old and new—showed up, and I found myself among a handful of people in my age group.

Nice people, I thought, happy I'd come to this event. But as for eligible men, no one stood out.

At that moment, a pleasant-looking man about my age came into the room. He was tall, casually dressed, but walked with perfect posture and seemed to know many of the oldies in the group.

Without hesitation, he came up and extended his hand, "Hi, I'm David," he said smiling. "Been a member here since I retired and I want to welcome you." I noticed the wedding band on his hand. *Well, he and his wife could still be friends*, I supposed.

He liked to talk, and in a short period of time I learned a lot about him and his family. . .particularly his son who played football for the Naval Academy in Annapolis, Maryland.

"What do *you* do?" he asked, as an afterthought. I told him I was an English teacher, but in my twenties had dated a midshipman, so was familiar with the Naval Academy.

"No kidding! What was his name? I have a lot of friends who went to Annapolis." When I mentioned 'Bill Rogers,' he cocked his head, wrinkled his brow as though trying to recall the person, then, "That name sounds familiar, but can't place him. Nope, doesn't ring a bell," he said. "Sorry." And with that, my new friend crossed the room to welcome another newbie.

Within seconds, another gentleman, also about our age, came over to me. "Hi, I'm Jim. Couldn't help overhear you and David. . .you mentioned a Bill Rogers who went to the Naval Academy?" "Yes, I did." "Well, I work with a Bill Rogers who did indeed graduate from the Naval Academy. Great guy, divorced, lives not too far from here, but don't know much else about him. We rarely mix work with our private lives, but it's probably the same Bill Rogers."

"Well, next time you see him, ask if he remembers Kate Arnold. . .Arnold was my maiden name. Let me know."

After church I headed home. Alone. So I'd made a friendly connection, and a possible reconnect. That was nice. It would take time for anything more to happen—if it was going to. At my age, I guessed there were no guarantees someone would come along again.

The following week, I saw Jim and his wife hurrying to catch up with me after Mass. "Hey Kate," he called out, "when I asked Bill if he remembered a Kate Arnold, he said, *of course I remember her, how do you know her*? And when I told him about our meeting at church, he said, *Yep, we were an item back then. For two years.*"

I smiled, glad he remembered me.

"I pressed him a bit further," Jim added, "and asked him what happened. . .said something about that *Catholic thing.*"

Jim had a gleam in his eye and was smiling. "He asked all about you. . .I told him I'd just met you and didn't know much about your life now, but he seemed eager to get in touch—hope you don't mind—I gave him your phone number since you'd allowed it to be published in the church directory and it was public. Was that okay?"

It was, and I said so.

Jim's wife was tugging at his sleeve. "Honey, we'll be late meeting the kids for lunch. He does things like this all the time," she said, addressing me with a smile, "a regular cupid."

As they walked away he called over his shoulder, "Bill says he'll be in touch. I should tell you that—" he winked and smiled, "—he seems to be in good shape for his age. Hope he calls."

As he walked away, I took a deep breath. I'd been polite when I'd said it was okay he'd given out my phone number. But I felt. . .uneasy. . .and I thought, *Thanks a bunch, Mr. Matchmaker.*

CHAPTER FIVE

Bill

"KATE?" the voice on the other end of the phone sounded familiar but I couldn't place it.

"This is she," I answered.

"I want to make sure I have the right Kate," the voice said. "Are you the Kate who was once the shuffleboard champion at the Naval Academy? The Kate who fell into the drink in front of the Admiral one Sunday at the same Naval Academy? The Kate who always made me ask the musicians to play 'Goodnight Sweetheart' *just once more,* at every dance?"

"Bill!"

"You're still crazy!" I tossed back, "But it's good to hear your voice. How are you?"

"I'm fine. It's been a long time and I'd like to see you, Kate. How about next Tuesday?"

Well that was sudden. I opened my mouth to say something like, "Let me check my calendar," but instead I said, "I can arrange it. Where?"

"Do you still have auburn hair that you pull up into a chignon, but that I like better when you let it down?"

Okay, stay centered, I thought. "Where do you want to meet, Mr. Fresh? And no, I cut my long hair years ago. Too much work, but I think you'll still recognize me."

"How about Da Domenico's Restaurant? Do you know where it is?"

"I do."

"Okay, twelve thirty, next Tuesday then. I work nearby and will have them save my table," he added. "I'll meet you inside."

I paused. It sounded more like an order than a

suggestion, but I agreed. "I'll be there."

"Looking forward to seeing you, Kate. *Ciao!*"

So, he's still working. . .has his favorite table at a pricy restaurant. . .what else? It would be an interesting lunch. And I had to admit, I was looking forward to seeing him, too.

Don't get ahead of yourself, I thought. *Forty years is a long time.*

I felt a little awkward walking into the restaurant alone, but what the heck, I had to face the reality that I *was* alone. I didn't see anyone standing nearby who resembled a forty-year-*older,* trim male with dark brown—or gray—hair. A moment later, the *maître d'* approached and asked if I was Miss Kate, waiting for Mr. Rogers.

"Yes, I am."

"He called to say his meeting is running overtime and he might be a few minutes late. He asked that I please seat you, so if you will follow me?

He led me to a round table in a quiet corner away from

the busy dining room. About five minutes later, I saw him come through the door—no mistaking Bill—exchange words with the *maître d'*, give him that "old buddy" pat on the shoulder, and walk towards the table where I was sitting. The trim figure I remembered was gone, but he seemed to be in good shape. He had a full head of beautiful, wavy, silver hair. . . a definite contrast to the dark brown military cut I remembered.

The years had obviously transformed "Rah! Rah! Joe College." He walked with an air of confidence, and like someone used to being in authority. The young midshipman I once knew was long gone, but I liked what I saw in his place.

He had a big smile on his face as he reached the table. I had forgotten how genuinely happy his smile always was. He stood there for a moment, just smiling at me, not saying a word, then sat down, reached across the table, and took both of my hands in his.

Well, this is nice. . . .

"You're just as I remember you," he said, with a tone

of nostalgia in his voice. "And you're not fat! Everyone else is fat! How did you manage to keep your figure?"

"I guess chasing five kids around plus doing a lot of gardening, I didn't need to work at it."

"You have five kids?"

"Yes, after my short-lived career."

"I have five kids, too."

As we bought each other up to date, sometimes in detail, we found amazing similarities in our lives. We both married within a year of each other and both had five children.

When I asked, "Where do you live?" I found he was less than fifteen minutes from my place. Incredible! His widowed sister lived with him; it had been a temporary arrangement at first, but since she traveled so much, it made more sense for her to stay there indefinitely. He cooked, she cleaned up. Seemed to work.

I told him I'd recently purchased my house and even though I'd made great headway, I was still a bit over-whelmed by what remained to be done with it.

"Call me, if you need advice or help," he said, "I've moved so many times I can do anything with a house."

He sounded sincere. I wasn't sure, however, if I was ready to take him up on the offer of help. . .and advice.

He ordered a carafe of wine and then suggested an item or two from the menu. The talk came easily and I allowed him to do most of it. After all, I wanted to know what had happened to him after our last date all those years ago.

And then, without hesitation, he shared his medical history with me. It involved a bout with cancer, radical surgery done years before, which had a dramatic effect on his relationships. "Because of the surgery, women are reluctant to date me," he said, "and I don't want to remarry."

I felt badly about it for him; he was such a fun loving, outgoing, romantic guy. It must have been a difficult decision for such a young man, but he was alive and healthy now.

"I'm so sorry you had to deal with that," I said, "but your limitations wouldn't bother. . ." I left the "me" unsaid, too forward for a first lunch, "everyone." And then to lighten the somber revelation, I changed the subject.

"First, I *did not* fall into the drink that Sunday during boating exercises. My date was distracted, and allowed the boom to knock me into the water. And it was the *Admiral* who reached out to pull me in!"

"Boy, was that embarrassing," he said with a laugh.

We found many other times and incidents to laugh about, as well.

All those years ago, Bill had been a clown, a brilliant musician, a fun guy, a devil, an entrepreneur, a really nice person. Although I always looked forward to an invitation from him, I was also dating one or two of the "men on campus" as they were called back then.

Some years after Bill and I had gone our separate ways, I'd married one of them.

It was a long lunch and he needed to get back to his office. I thanked him for the lunch and told him to drop by if he was in the neighborhood.

He walked me to my car and when he saw it, asked, "Is this yours?"

"Yes, why?" "Well, that's mine next to it."

We both started to laugh: we were both driving the same make and model, his black, mine grey.

I unlocked my door and he opened it for me, and leaned in to give me a gentle kiss on the cheek good-bye.

I didn't ask him why his letters had suddenly stopped forty years ago, without any explanation.

Nor did I tell him that I had saved the others.

As I slowly drove away, I watched as he zoomed off in the other direction. I smiled. *Still the old, full-speed-ahead Bill.* We had covered a lot of territory that afternoon and decided to 'keep in touch,' but I wasn't sure I would hear from him again.

A few days later, my brother came by for dinner.

"Hey, Sis, you expecting someone?" he called out from the porch as I heard a car pull into my wide driveway.

"No, just you." I wiped my hands on the kitchen towel and went out to see who it might be. "Maybe someone's lost," I said, as I headed out the door. "Well, whoever it is must have been here before," he said. . ."seems to know his way around. . .charged in, turned the car around and is parking it. Do you recognize the car?"

I did.

"I see you found my place," I said, as Bill came bounding out of his car. "Come in and meet my brother."

I introduced them, then said to Bill, "I'm about to grill a couple steaks, would you like to join us? I have plenty."

"No, no, I just wanted to see where you lived, don't want to interfere with your visit." "Well, at least come in and have a cool drink with us. It's so hot!"

He followed me in and offered to help. When I told him I was having a martini, he said, "Then, I'll have one too," and proceeded to make it for himself. When he saw the two massive rib-eye steaks on the counter he showed me how to rub them with sugar before grilling to seal in the juice and flavor.

With drinks in hand, we joined my brother on the porch. It did not take much prodding to convince Bill to stay for supper. I excused myself to put the steaks on the already hot grill and left the two of them chatting.

Within moments, though, Bill was standing beside me. I realized sweat was pouring down my face. I had no make up on and felt rather grubby. *Well,* I thought, *he came without calling and this is how I sometimes look on a hot day after work.*

Apparently my appearance didn't bother him, because in less than a minute he was standing so close to me I thought he'd fall onto the grill. He took the tongs as I moved away from him, and whispered in my ear, "You're beautiful, and you smell good, too."

He flipped the steaks over before I thought they were finished, and told me, "they'll continue to cook after you take them off." I was dying to know what this once laid back friend did in the military. Another visit was definitely in order.

While Bill was washing his hands, I put the food on the table. When he came back out, he looked around the porch, patted the dog and sat down in the chair I pointed to.

"What a great porch," he said. "I like to eat outside!"

My brother was unusually quiet, probably storing observations. . . .a habit he'd developed from childhood. Although ten years younger, Archie envisioned himself as my protector and I was a little concerned about what he would have to say about this evening.

We finished a very pleasant dinner and Bill offered to help clean up. "Absolutely not!" I told him. "Then I'll be on my way and let you have some quality time with your brother," he said, thanking me profusely for the delicious meal.

He apologized for barging in and interrupting our visit, said he was sorry he hadn't called first but happened to be nearby and just took a chance I was home.

I walked him to his car, while Archie stayed behind. "Had a great evening," he said, "I'll have you over and fix dinner for you next time April goes on one of her trips. . .I like to cook."

He gave me a hug, nodded at my brother on the porch. "I'll kiss you in private, later," he whispered, and jumped in his car.

I watched as he tore down the long driveway, creating a breeze that rustled the shrubs on that hot, still summer night.

Back at the house, my brother was not impressed. "That guy is full of it," he said. . ."probably had a girl in every port." Then, mockingly, *"You're beautiful, and you smell good!"* Yeah, you must have smelled great, Kate. Sweaty, smoky, end of the day, 90 degrees! You'd better watch him. He's coming on strong really fast."

I smiled to myself. . .*you don't have to worry about him, little brother. Not with his medical history.*

One week later, Bill invited me out to dinner at another very nice restaurant.

A few days after that, he popped by again, unannounced. When I opened the door for him I noticed he was limping.

"What's wrong?"

"I have a big splinter in my foot and can't get it out."

"Let me see it," I asked, and within a second, he had his shoe off. "Why didn't you let your sister try?"

"Because she can't see worth a damn, and besides, I wanted *you* to do it. With all those kids you probably had lots of experience with splinters."

It was a nasty looking thing, much larger than a little splinter and I felt he should go to the ER. But no, *I* had to get the thing out for him.

After cleansing the area with some Betadine I was able to extract the fragment of wood. I put a squirt of Neosporin ointment on the wound and covered the area with a large Band-Aid. "Keep clean socks on," I told him, "and go to the doctor if it looks infected."

Two weeks later, he called and asked if he could come by for a few minutes. I was available so told him to come on over.

"How's your foot?" I asked as we settled on the porch again, this time with iced tea.

"It's fine, all healed."

After a few moments of silence he said, "It's the *other* wound that never healed. I want to talk to you about it."

"Where is it?" I asked, thinking perhaps he meant an

injury incurred in the military.

He put his hand over his heart. "Here," he said. "It got broken forty years ago and never healed."

I didn't know what to say.

He got up, crossed the porch, and sat down beside me.

"Do you remember that last summer I saw you. . .before I went home to visit my parents for two weeks? Well, I told my mother that I was going to ask you to marry me the following June, after graduation."

I couldn't believe what I was hearing; he and I never talked about marriage, or even love! I was not aware he had such feelings.

Bill continued, "When I told my mother you were a Catholic, she was adamant. Her exact words were, "We come from generations of New England WASPS, and we *do not* marry Catholics! I forbid it."

"She told me I was not to see you again, or even call or write you. 'That's how you break it off,' she said."

He shook his head, then lowered it. "I did what my mother told me to do," he said, with his head bent. "That's the way it was back then. I'm so sorry."

He was right. In those days, prejudice ran deep between Catholics and Protestants marrying.

Bill took my hand and held it. Looking at me, he said in a firm voice, "But I never fully got over you, I never forgot you. You were my first love."

I was overwhelmed by this revelation.

While I always looked forward to seeing him those two years we dated, I was not in love with him, and had no idea that he might have been in love with me. He was a fun date, a good dancer, handsome, charming, and we enjoyed kissing, but in love, I didn't think so.

I'd never thought of him as an intellectual, though he was bright and capable.

I shifted the subject slightly, asking him to tell me more about his life after we'd. . .lost touch.

That calmed things down, and he sat back, sipped his iced tea, and filled me in: He'd risen through the ranks, commanded more than one ship, became an authority in his specialty, which he then taught at Post Graduate School and for years, back at the Naval Academy.

After he retired, he'd run alumni and civic groups. . .always on the run, always going somewhere, always doing something. *No surprise to me, as he was a born leader.*

As he left that afternoon, he stepped close to me for that promised private kiss.

How strange and wonderful it felt to kiss a man who'd just called me his first love—and who finished the visit with, "I've wondered for years after my wife and I split, if there was a chance I would ever find you. And then David called. I couldn't believe it!"

Bill's spontaneous visits became routine and I got used to them. He soon became a fixture in my home and would drop by whenever, if just to play the piano. We enjoyed each other's company, and found we could talk about a variety of subjects—from books and films, to politics and history. Over time, he revealed little things about himself to me.

"Things I can't tell anyone else," he would say.

Once, he laughingly said he imagined that talking to me was like being a Catholic going to confession. "You get it out of you and you feel better. It's a good thing."

I often wondered why we were re-connected so late in life. Maybe there was a reason, a purpose. It's always been my belief that everything happens for a reason.

Bill was a fun person, and affectionate. His sense of humor was contagious and he became my best friend. It did not matter to me that we did not have an intimate physical relationship. He filled a void in my life and cared about my welfare. He was there if I needed him, often seeing a need or problem before I did, and I was there for him.

As the months progressed, we began to travel together, driving up one coast and down the other. We cruised to Alaska, spent a week in Key West, and danced wherever there was music. He simply loved life.

That was it, I thought. The reason we'd been brought back together—at least from my perspective. A lost love and a failed relationship had taken a lot of the life out of me.

Bill taught me what it was to be alive again.

I knew I was not the most important person in his life, and that was okay. He adored his grandkids and was close to his five children. But I *was* important to him.

One day he startled me.

"I know we were related in another life," he spurted out, "and that we'll see each other again in the next life. I'm sure there's some kind of bond between us."

This surprised me, as he'd never spoken much about his beliefs or his spirituality.

Something inside me said, *Take notice of this. It's important.* I had no idea why we were suddenly alluding to death.

Then I found out.

Not long after, Bill's cancer reared its ugly head again. We didn't shy away from talking about death, and one day we decided that whomever of us went first, he or she would be there to greet the other when they arrived.

When it became obvious months later that he was going to be the first to go, I found it more difficult than he did. As I sat beside him on one of his waning days, he smiled at me and said, "You know, Kate, I'm actually looking forward to my new adventure."

I believed he was.

One day, toward the end, he said, "My door is open, just walk in anytime, day or night. I want you to come whenever you can."

Another day, he called and asked me to make a certain dish for him then proceeded to tell me exactly what to put in and how to make it. It made me smile, as I had probably taught him how to make that particular dish. His culinary ability had dramatically improved since we'd reconnected, and he liked to tell people, "Thanks to Kate who taught me all I know." So, I followed his directions and brought it to him.

He even had seconds that evening, thanking me over and over, "This is so delicious."

Though he was usually talkative, that evening, he sat quietly, as his sister and I cleared the table. While in the kitchen, I heard him slide his chair away from the table, and then heard the motor on the chair lift start. I continued loading the dishwasher and assumed he was going to the bathroom, but why didn't he use the one on the same floor?

When I stepped back into the dining room, his sister was looking at me with tears in her eyes.

"He couldn't say good-bye to you," she said. "He's gone up to his room."

I felt shaken. *This man who is so full of life cannot be leaving us.*

After she and I finished cleaning up, I said good-bye to her and left. *I'll come by in a couple of days,* I thought.

I got into my car and sat there for a moment. Too sad to think, I turned on the radio, only to hear these words being sung. . ."Softly, as I leave you. . ." and started to cry.

Why couldn't he say good-bye to me tonight?

Bill died two days later.

I attended his funeral at the Naval Academy one month later but left the reception early.

Tearfully, I got into my car for the drive home and again, turned the radio on to block any more sad thoughts.

I couldn't believe what they were playing. "Softly, as I

leave you. . ." and I realized Bill *was* saying good-bye after all.

Our years' long relationship was not a marriage, but my loss was deep and painful. We were too different in many ways to ever marry, but the relationship was good for us and we'd made each other happy.

I headed back home filled with not only a deep sadness, but with a feeling of emptiness. . .and the realization that I was alone once more.

As I crossed the Severn River, leaving behind the remains of someone very dear to me, I suddenly felt disconnected. Another part of my life was gone, but the memories would never leave me.

"Somewhere," I said out loud, "when I have grieved sufficiently, I will find a love that combines the friendships I have lost *and* the physical love that I desire." I hoped there was still time.

CHAPTER SIX

Missteps and New Beginnings

I MISSED BILL'S CHEERFUL voice on the phone. And whenever a car pulled into my driveway I expected to see him jump out and give me a big hug.

When I told my friends of his passing, they were sad. They had come to know Bill because he would often drop by for a visit anytime he knew a few of them were coming to my home for lunch. Because of his predictable visits I would always have a place set for him, and if he wasn't there... they would ask where he was. Everyone had found him that entertaining.

To cheer me up, my friends from Bethany Beach, three hours away, suggested I get away for a few days and come down for a visit. It seemed like a good idea to spend time walking the beach in the company of caring people, and I accepted.

Maybe, I thought, it's *time to put to rest this whole silly idea of looking for a partner.* Especially at my age—now past seventy. After all, with each passing year, the chances of finding someone whose life and heart would connect with mine seemed to be growing slimmer and slimmer.

A week later, I packed an overnight bag and headed for the beach, feeling an old, familiar love for the ocean rise in me as I crossed the Chesapeake Bay bridge to the Eastern Shore of Maryland. By midday, six of us were in the lobby of "Victoria by the Sea." It was good to get together with the gang for lunch at a restaurant and not be cooking.

We were close friends as students and continued to stay

close after we graduated. For years, several of us met every month for lunch or dinner. . .we were more like family than friends and were always there for one another.

But gradually, our lives had changed. We'd retired, were widowed, got divorced, moved away. . .but still, we'd continued to keep in touch, and our getting together at the beach was always a treat.

The restaurant was our favorite meeting place when we came down to Bethany, and as we filed into the large bright dining room, everyone headed for a chair.

"Kate, you sit here," Joan said, as she pulled out an armchair that would give me a view. "*We* see the ocean all the time."

As I sank into the deep, padded chair, I looked out at the lovely ocean and felt at peace. I was in the company of women I considered to be not only lifelong friends, but truly, family.

Over the course of lunch, my friends filled the conversation with laughter and stories and how much they loved their lives in this beach town.

"Kate, you need to move here and join us. We know you'll enjoy living here."

I knew they meant it, but would this be enough for me the rest of my life? Why did I want something more?

Most of them had moved here after finding themselves single again, and none of them had remarried. In fact, they liked their singleness. . .maybe because they had each other.

I, on the other hand, preferred having a partner. This I knew. Why would this desire not leave me, even after all my losses?

Driving home the next day, I weighed the pros and cons of living in Bethany.

No. I was not ready for the single life. I decided I should at least give online dating another try. Though it still did not sit well with me, what could it hurt?

Shortly after my return home, I re-activated my Senior Match.com account. If the profiles looked good, I would answer the email.

Occasionally, I initiated the contact. After a few weeks of back-and-forth emails, one or the other would suggest a phone call. That was not a sure sign either. After a while, I realized it was better to just meet: If there was no chemistry, I'd know immediately, and move on.

I stayed with Match for almost a year. . .off and on. During that time, I did meet some interesting men. When one told me he was interested in a "casual relationship" I thought, *Good. No pressure.* Casual, to me, meant a movie, glass of wine, a cup of coffee, small talk, lunch, or a dutch dinner. That would be fine. I'd get to know him and then see where it went.

It soon became apparent, however, that to him *casual* meant casual *sex.* No thank you.

There were other men who came along and seemed great at first. Then, I realized, most of them had too much baggage. If they were divorced, it was often apparent the divorce had taken its toll and they were not ready for another round. No woman on a date needs to hear pent-up anger directed towards women in general.

There were other men, very nice, but still, not for me.

Maybe I was just driving myself crazy, and there was

no one out there. Why would this urge to love and be loved not just leave me alone?

Then I met several very nice widowers. Most of them wanted to talk about their late wives. I did not qualify as a therapist. I did not go on Match.com to be a buddy, either. One talked non-stop about his deceased wife, detailing every trip they took, little habits of hers, funny things she would say or do, and told me I reminded him of her. He definitely needed grief counseling.

Another kept a blown up photo of his late wife taped to the dashboard of his car, and continually referred to her as, "my sweetie," as he would periodically blow a kiss to her as we were driving along.

After a while, I began to feel that I was not supposed to ever again meet a man that could be mine. I knew it was late in life but weren't any of those men willing to start over or at least enjoy the remainder of their lives with another woman?

Despite the fact that I knew at least five women who had met the love of their life online and were now married to them, I realized I did not have the patience or expertise to wade through this sad, lonely, or angry group of men to find my eternal love.

And so, I cancelled my subscription to Match.com. But I continued to pray for a companion, a partner, someone I—hopefully—could love, and who would love me back.

After I decided to give it a rest, classes at a local university took up two days of my week. In addition, I was working part time, and had agreed to help on a busy committee at my new church. I really did not have time for romance anyway.

In fact I hardly had time for my friends lately, and that disturbed me, so when I saw a message from my friend Rose on my machine, I returned the call right away. Rose and I had met years ago while graduate students at Georgetown and had traveled together several times. Though she was a few years older, we seemed to click and we traveled well together.

I wondered what she had on her mind now.

Rose was tall for a woman. Her long dark hair was

now blended with some grey but her lovely brown eyes still resembled precious stones. Her nails were always polished, and she dressed with an air of fashion. And she had never been married. She wasn't always single, but never married.

Before time got away from me, I dialed her number.

"Kate, there's a wonderful tour of Italy coming up this spring." She was so excited her words were running together. "And I'll go if you will!" Rose spoke Italian, and traveling with someone who spoke the language would be a plus. Italy was high on my bucket list, so I told her I'd think about it and get back to her.

But I had to do more than *think* about it.

There was still some money in my investment portfolio but I hated to touch it. I also had a small savings account for emergencies, but the trip would deplete it.

Money, or the lack of it, had recently been an issue in my life but it was not my god. As long as I could survive, be independent, and still work, I did not feel bound to it.

The rationalizing went on for a few days. I told myself that I was not likely to find a man who was willing to support me, but at the same time, there was no time like the present. Why wait? I decided to dip into the funds and take what I needed for the trip of a lifetime.

Since Italy was four months away, I had ample time to not only prepare for it, but to keep my mind occupied with something positive and cheerful in the meantime.

It was also time for my yearly visit with Lia, the astrologer and psychic with whom I had become a good friend. Twice a year I checked in with her for a reading.

What would my astrological chart dictate for the coming months? Would this be a propitious time for me to travel? What else was on the horizon? What did I need to know to stay focused? Was there anything to watch out for, or postpone?

Her readings, while not carved in stone, had proven to be a vital guideline to me and I looked forward to each session.

Her first words surprised me. "Are you in a new relationship?" she asked. "No, not at all," I answered. "Well, the cards are showing me that you are, or are going to be, in a loving, caring, intimate, committed relationship."

"Lia!" I interrupted, "I would love to have a partner, someone in my life, but no way am I marrying again."

"Well, then you will be living with him because I see you together. . .they would not have shown me this if it was not so."

"I don't know *anyone* I would marry," I told her.

"Well, then you haven't met him yet, but you will know who it is by the end of summer."

When she 'saw' me traveling to Italy, I asked her if I was going to meet this new man there. "No, you're not going to meet him in Italy. . . but closer to home."

"They're showing me a very large clock," she added, "and a body of water. . .looks like a river. These are signs by which you'll recognize him. I don't know what that means. . .time for a cruise maybe? Maybe that's where you'll meet him, on a cruise."

"They're telling me that when you see these signs around him, you will know."

She continued with other life information, which

proved helpful. . .but I tucked the other part of the reading away and tried to forget about it. No use waiting around. Preparing for the upcoming trip in a few months took precedence over other things and I concentrated on work, classes, and Italy.

Time flew by and suddenly, the day was upon us.

We were flying out of Dulles, and since Rose lived at a distance, we decided to meet at the airport. I arrived at the designated time and waited for her in Lufthansa's boarding area. Sixty, thirty, then fifteen minutes before boarding. . . .still no Rose.

Suddenly I realized I needed some papers that were in my carry-on and I leaned over to open it, but couldn't budge the zipper. The more I tugged at it the more frozen it became. On my last overseas trip, TSA had broken the zipper but I had had it repaired. Or so I'd thought.

Anxious, I looked around for my travel companion, but still, no sign of her. I'd give it one more try and then ask for help—surely someone could dislodge the darned thing.

Bent over the carry-on, I gave the zipper one strong

pull, lost my balance and started to teeter sideways. Almost instantly, I felt a steadying hand on my arm and looked up into the face of a very tall man who was bending over me.

Not only tall, but nice looking.

"Always glad to help a damsel in distress," he said, as he pulled me to my feet.

Then he looked at the bag. "Let me see that thing,"— and he gave the zipper one strong jerk. With that, it slid open.

He stood up and put his hand out, "I'm Jack," he said, with a smile. "You had something stuck in it. . .it's not broken."

He must have been reading my mind, I thought. I took his offered hand, "Kate Murphy," and smiled back. "I can't thank you enough."

"So, where are you going?" he asked.

"Italy. I'm catching up with a tour group from my Alma Mater that left earlier."

"Flying alone?"

"No, but I don't know where my travel partner

is. . .probably getting something to eat, or looking in the shops. She always shows up just in time to board."

"*She*?" He smiled again.

I could get used to that smile.

"And you?" I asked, redirecting. "Is your wife traveling with you?" I'd noticed the wedding band on his hand.

"No, she's deceased. . .passed away two years ago."

"Oh, I'm sorry," I offered, and quickly erased the smile off my face. Better to not ask any more questions.

"She was sick a long time," he volunteered. "I'm relieved for her, that she's out of the pain she was in, but I don't like to be in the house alone, so I travel when I'm not working."

And then to change the subject he added, "Don't worry, seasoned travelers know how much time they have and if your friend misses the flight, I'll see you get to your destination. I'm traveling with the same group and we'll probably be seeing a lot of each other the next two weeks."

Now this was a pleasant surprise.

A few minutes later, a voice came over the loudspeaker:

"Flight 148 to Milan will be boarding at Gate 13 in ten minutes. "

Where *was* Rose? I began walking away from the area, with carry-on in tow, hoping to see her among the wave of people scurrying to make their own flights. And there she was! Hurrying up the walkway toward us, dragging a huge purse and an even heavier carry-on. I wondered how she ever ran a business. Organized chaos at its finest.

We reached the boarding area with just enough time to introduce Rose and Jack. Waiting in line to board, they began to chat, and I recognized the subliminal interactions between them. They not only *looked* like a couple, they looked like the *perfect* couple. Tall, dark Rose. . .and tall, silver haired, distinguished looking Jack.

My momentary sense of excitement waned.

I could tell there was some chemistry on her part by the way she looked at Jack when he was not aware, and by the way she coyly lowered her head when he told her she was a "beautiful woman." Then, without asking, he said, "Here, let me take that," and he relieved her of her heavy carry-on.

Well, well, Rose, I thought, *maybe this time you lucked out. My loss.*

I guess that was that with Jack. He wasn't looking for me, he was looking for someone. Anyone. And that was not what I was looking for.

CHAPTER SEVEN

Italy

WE BOARDED THE JUMBO JET without incident—or almost.

Some passengers were directed to the left side of the massive plane, some to the right. It was here we lost track of Jack.

After wending our way down the aisle, Rose and I began the daunting task of getting settled in our seats. Carry-ons were stored above, essentials under the seat. The disinfectant wipes came out before we sat down and we cleaned everything in sight. We had been too busy getting settled to look around and find where Jack was sitting, but out of the corner of my eye, *and pretending not to notice,* I saw my travel buddy looking around for him.

Dinner was a bit above our expectations, and we both commented on the fact that this was a classy flight. But I was not in the mood for a movie, so I pulled out our tour manual and went over the names of those listed; the only names I recognized were ours and Jack's.

And then I noticed something I had previously missed.

I knew Rose and I were the only single women in the group, now I saw there were *two single* males as well. That could be interesting. Hmm. . . .

Don't go there, Kate. Single only means they are traveling alone. It does not always mean they are "single," as in available.

Since we'd already met one of them, I wondered who the other one was.

About ten o'clock U.S. time, I felt tired enough to retire and looked forward to getting some—if not a good night's—sleep. After a brief trip to the bathroom and 10 mg of Ambien, I slid beneath my own travel blanket, affixed my eye-mask, leaned back on the slightly reclined seat, and attempted to relax.

Rose immediately fell asleep. Thank heaven, as I was not in the mood for chit-chat. I envied those who had no trouble sleeping. Their snoring gave them away.

I closed my eyes, thought pleasant thoughts, and did my best to fall asleep, but it didn't happen.

My mind kept taking me back to the handsome and thoughtful gentleman I'd just met. Or rather, *we'd* just met. Since Rose had a tendency to be assertive and I did not, I half-resigned myself to becoming a third wheel.

In five hours, I watched the sun come up over the horizon, and wondered how I would manage this lovely whole new day without *any* sleep.

Our arrival in Milan was exciting, and I soon found myself wide awake from the excitement. I gathered my luggage, only to find my travel companion had miraculously disappeared. Where were the others? Where was our guide?

I was getting a little antsy by now and as I turned around to look for Rose I saw both Rose and Jack heading toward me. . .each coming from a different direction.

"Good morning ladies!" Jack's bubbly voice and demeanor energized me again, and almost at once I forgot how tired I was. Apparently *he* had slept. "How did you fare during the night?" he asked.

"I barely dozed," I sighed.

"Don't worry, you'll have plenty of time to take a nap before the grand reception this evening." Jack's smile, as much as his words, reassured me, and I felt better.

Outside the terminal, after we'd retrieved our luggage, I was glad Jack had stuck with us. I was jet-lagged and a bit foggy.

"Come on," he nudged my arm gently. "I think I see our limo. . .has a *Georgetown Tour Group* sign on it," and he headed toward the curb. "You two have all your bags? Need any help?"

I waited to see if he picked up Rose's bag again, but the tour guide had already grabbed it.

Once on the bus, our local guide introduced himself and said all we had to do was follow him. We recognized faces we had seen in the airport and on the plane but had no idea who among this small crowd would be our B&B buddy for the next fourteen days.

The short ride from the airport to the four-star Cavour Hotel took us along beautiful tree-lined streets, and blooming flowers that were a most pleasant welcome.

Once we arrived at the hotel it was only a matter of handing us our keys. Everything else had been done ahead of time.

Jack managed to find us before we left the lobby for our rooms. "See you two later," he said, looking over his shoulder and winking, as we headed for our respective rooms.

Rose and I unpacked, took a brief tour of the place, then a short walk around the block before heading back to our delightful room and my long awaited nap. Afraid I'd oversleep, I was relieved when Rose assured me that her up-to-date electronic device would wake us up...

...and it did, but with barely enough time to shower,

dress and make it downstairs for the tail end of the cocktail party.

As we came down the stairs, I spotted Jack talking to several couples. We had time for a glass of wine but not enough time to meet the others. In a few minutes, the concierge advised us that the taxis would be here in five minutes to take us to Don Carlos, one of Milan's finest restaurants. The only problem was that there were more of us than there were available taxies.

"You must not be late for the reservation or they will give your table away," the excited concierge kept repeating, and we believed him.

Jack looked unperturbed. "I'm going to walk. Would you ladies care to join me? It's only a few blocks away, and we'll be there sooner than if we waited for another taxi."

How could we refuse? A few more guests joined our small party and Jack led the way. High heels and all, we walked the few fun blocks.

We found our assigned seats at the reserved tables in the restaurant's gorgeous old world dining room. The silk wallpaper was covered with portraits of important people, most of whom we were familiar with. The tables were lit with candles and soft music was playing. The house wine would have cost a fortune in the States. So delightful!

Ah, romantic Italy! And here I was sitting with. . .another woman. A dear friend, but still, not very romantic.

Fortunately, the two other couples seated at our table were fun. The conversation was lively, and we had some interesting things in common. But occasionally, Rose and I carefully scanned the room to see if we could find the other single man.

"I think that must be him at the next table," Rose quietly said, and I cautiously looked in that direction.

The man we'd zeroed in on seemed about our age, nice looking guy, but wasn't doing much talking, just listening. A bit of a contrast to Jack. It was well known that Rose had no trouble opening a conversation with a stranger so I felt it would only be a matter of time until she checked this other guy out more thoroughly.

After dinner we left the restaurant but stood out front watching the people go by. Aware that Milan was the fashion center of the world, what better place to watch a fashion show. Glued to the passing scene, I failed to notice Jack standing right next to us.

And next to him, was the *other single man*. It hadn't taken long for the singles to find each other. . .probably in self defense. . .safety in numbers, or something like that.

"Hi, ladies," Jack greeted us. "I'd like you to meet Pete. He's the other loner in the group. Thought we'd have a little nightcap. Care to join us?"

"We'd love to," Rose and I answered, without thinking about it for more than a second. The four of us then walked the short distance to an outdoor, covered mall the guys had found earlier in the day. Making small talk, we sipped *limoncello* with our make- believe dates in a quaint little area outside a busy restaurant.

It would be the first of many such evenings.

The following day, we toured Museo del Teatro alla Scala, and were so awed at the display of elaborate costumes the opera stars wore in live productions, some weighing close to fifty or more pounds, that we couldn't wait for that evening's production of Turandot.

Since our hotel was within walking distance of La Scala, Rose and I decided to linger a while after the performance. We wanted to get a closer look at the incredibly fashionable women who walked down the famous red carpet of La Scala's Opera House, and out to their waiting limos or taxi's. .

One more beautiful than the other. . . .what a sight! Only in Milan.

And who was watching this as well? Yep, our two guys.

"Too late for a nightcap?" Jack asked, "we found another place, it's not that far, a block or two. . .how about it?" The weather was balmy and a walk would have felt good after sitting for so long. "I'd love to," I said. Rose hesitated a moment, looked at her watch. . .then, "not for me tonight, it's been a long day and we'll be up early. Think I'm ready to turn in."

"Well, how about dinner tomorrow, then. We're on our own for lunch *and* dinner you know." Without waiting for an answer, "Let's meet in the lobby about six and we'll walk on over. Found another nice place. Think you'll like it." We all agreed.

I had a feeling Rose preferred to sit next to Jack, but since I enjoyed both the guys, it didn't matter who I sat next to. *I'll let her choose a seat first when we get there*, I said to myself.

Though the truth was, while I was definitely attracted to Jack, it was not in a romantic way. I just felt comfortable around him, maybe *safe* was the right word.

In less time than I expected, we arrived. "Here we are," Jack announced as we walked into a huge mall surrounded with so many shops it would take a week to visit them all.

We had no trouble being seated out front after refusing to be seated in a dark corner of the back room where the wait staff must have thought we wanted a romantic spot. I had to stifle a smile when he realized we weren't dates, but tourists.

After the waiter took our drink orders, I continued to look with awe at my surroundings, and was so consumed by the sheer space of this huge covered mall that I hadn't noticed who was sitting where. Our drinks arrived and as we made a toast, I saw that Rose had seated herself as close to Jack as she could. . .as though there wasn't enough room in this huge place. It seemed almost amusing.

Conversation flowed easily during the evening, and we found it a pleasant diversion from the rest of the tour. During a quiet moment, I noticed Pete looking from left to right, and up at the multiple-story-high building and the glass roof covering the largest mall I'd ever seen. He seemed to be taking it all in as if seeing it for the first time, when he said, "This is the only building in Italy that we never bombed."

He was referring to World War II, of course. I had never even thought about that. And here we were sitting in a sacred place in a country that I loved.

"Does it have a name?" I asked. *Galleria Vittorio*

Emanuele II. I wondered what other knowledge he harbored in his quiet head.

Dinner was reasonable compared to the fine dining we had previously experienced. A relief, since Rose and I decided we would pay our own bill. It would take the pressure off the guys and make things more comfortable.

As Rose and I pulled out our credit cards, Jack and Pete both said, "This doesn't feel right, we should be paying." "No, this is more comfortable," I said. Rose added, "We planned on paying our own way, makes it easier for everyone."

It kept the relationship where we wanted it. . .I thought.

In fact, after a few days, regrouping for a nightcap became our evening ritual. No matter which city we were staying in, the four of us would find a place for our *limoncello* nightcap.

Three of us made a game of our togetherness—the two men and I. Rose took it more seriously.

One evening, Pete asked me with a straight face, "Whose wife are you tonight?"

"Well, I forget whose wife I was last night," I said. "Maybe I'll be yours tonight—or should I be Jack's? I don't know. I can't make up my mind!"

"That'll be fine," he answered, and we both laughed at our silliness.

Rose did not break a smile.

We went from Milan with our box seats at La Scala to Parma where we watched a local couple make cheese, then were escorted into a moldy underground storage room where they aged the unforgettable Parma hams. In Modena we toured the lofts where they made and stored balsamic vinegars. At lunch that day, we were treated to a sampling of different balsamic vinegars, some forty years old, one of which I ended up purchasing.

Wherever Rose and I were, the two guys were not far away.

During the day, Jack and Pete hung out together. But when evening came, it was always the four of us. . .sometimes others would ask to come along and we welcomed them. All seemed well, no apparent problems, until one day. . . .

Early that morning, we were driven to a cheese factory where we stood on cement floors for several hours observing a couple going through the steps of making cheese using a centuries' old method. By lunchtime we were more tired than hungry. Jack, who had been standing nearby as the demonstration came to an end, took my arm and said, "Let's go." We made a beeline for the pavilion where we knew a sumptuous lunch awaited us. The rest of the group followed at a more leisurely pace.

When he asked, "Where's Rose?" I thought he wanted us to wait for her.

"Oh, she often stays behind taking pictures," I said, "she'll catch up."

As we entered the pavilion, I asked him where he wanted to sit.

"I don't care where I sit," he answered, "as long as it's down." So we took the first two seats in front of us and waited for the rest of the group.

When Rose finally caught up, she found Jack sitting at the end of a long table, and I was sitting beside him. We had saved a place for her but it was next to me. By the look on her face, I felt she was annoyed about something.

That afternoon, back at our hotel room, Rose was unusually quiet as she and I carefully put our prized purchases of balsamic vinegar and cheese away... I sensed she was a bit down.

We had not walked very much that day as most of our time was spent standing and observing. I wanted to make sure there were no hard feelings where Jack was concerned. Maybe a walk might be in order.

"If you're not too tired," I said, smiling, "how about some leisurely window shopping before dinner? I noticed some lovely shops nearby yesterday."

"I'd like that," she answered, "they do have great shops here, and we haven't really had time to do any shopping yet. Give me a few minutes and I'll be ready."

Apparently all was well between us and in a few minutes I heard, "OK, let's go."

We were ooh-ing and ahh-ing in one of the more elegant dress shops when Rose said, "Look at this!" and showed me the label on a lovely expensive blue chiffon robe. *Made in Reggio Emilia.* "That's where we are," she said, apparently forgetting the lunch experience. The clothes were priced way beyond our means but it was worth the experience.

The unhurried browsing allowed for a pleasant, relaxing atmosphere where we made small talk, mostly about the tour.

Then, after a lull in our chatter, Rose said, in a rather *laissez faire* manner, "I think Pete's interested in you." I wondered where *that* came from. "Really? What gave you that impression?""Oh, just the way he looks at you and tries to sit next to you whenever he can. I saw both of you talking the other day, and it seemed to be a serious conversation."

I thought for a moment, and then recalled the incident. "Yes, we were, I was asking about his late wife, and what she died from. I could tell he was hesitant, and then was sorry

I'd asked. Told him I didn't mean to pry, was just interested. Then. . .he suddenly opened up."

"Pete said he doesn't like to talk about his wife because he's afraid people might think he's living in the past."

I knew from experience how important it is to talk about your loss, your memories, what you're afraid of. I wish I could have talked to someone years ago. . .but the subject was off limits and I had to keep it inside. You grieve forever that way.

"Some guys don't know how to talk about their feelings, so they make small talk. . .they make jokes, they pretend. . .or they don't talk at all. Maybe that's why he's so quiet."

"So, that's why I let him talk, Rose. And that's why he sits beside me, I guess he feels comfortable talking about something painful, and I listen and feel his pain."

She didn't respond, and in a few minutes she heaved a sigh, "It's always difficult to talk about pain," she said. "Come on, we'll be late for the cocktail party before dinner," and she headed for the door.

Our shopping spree was over.

"I'm glad Pete finally opened up about himself," I said, as we walked back toward the hotel. "He needed a little prodding, but I also learned a lot about him once he started talking. He's got a lot to say once he gets going."

"He has a great sense of humor, is well educated. . .has multiple degrees, and his work takes him around the world. Neat guy. Will be a good catch for the right person. . .when he's ready But. . .just. . .not my type. . .no chemistry there. Sorry Rose."

"Well, don't be surprised if he calls you after we get home," she countered. "One never *knows*. . ." she trailed off.

Good try Rose.

Our tour group had dinner together that evening, before breaking up into smaller groups that headed in various directions, since it was far too early to go to bed and there was literally nothing to do back at the hotel.

Several couples invited the four of us to join them, but we declined their invitation and followed our own plans.

128

Another delightful, entertaining, informative evening together, now in the beautiful city of Florence.

Back at the hotel, as Rose and I headed for the elevator, I heard Jack call out, "Tomorrow night at six, then? Meet us here in the lobby." Rose nodded her head 'yes' and blew the two guys a kiss.

"What was all that about?" I asked her.

"You were talking to someone when Pete and Jack asked if we would like to join them for dinner tomorrow. I told him we'd love to."

We had a full schedule the next day, but were on our own for dinner again.

And now we had *dates* for tomorrow evening, even though they were make believe. And even though I wasn't sure which one would be *mine,* it was a good feeling.

With so much to look forward to, I slept well that night.

I love breakfast, so always made sure I was in the dining room with ample time to enjoy it without having to rush. The selection was overwhelming and I was eyeing the assortment of melons, when suddenly a slice of ripe honeydew landed on my plate.

I turned to see Jack standing behind me.

"Decisions a little tough in the morning?" he said, with raised eyebrows and a devilish smile on his face. "Yesterday, you couldn't decide which sweet roll you wanted."

"I didn't see you yesterday," I said, "were you in the dining room for breakfast?"

"Uh huh. . .right behind you, but you were deep in conversation with the couple from Baltimore. And then you went into the other room to sit with Rose."

"Sorry, didn't mean to be rude. . .just didn't see you. . . and thanks for deciding which melon I *wanted* this morning. They all look so good I couldn't decide. . .can't wait to taste it."

I moved around the large serving table, scooped a spoonful of scrambled eggs onto my plate and looked up at Jack who was busy filling his own plate. "Think that's enough," I said to myself, out loud. And before heading to the table where Rose was having her second cup of 'wake up' coffee, I said to Jack, "Enjoy the day, looking forward to tonight."

"And you watch out for the taxies," he answered back, "please, try to stay on the *sidewalk.*"

Jack was referring to an incident that happened a few days before when our group was heading to Al Trebbio, a lovely small restaurant around the corner from our hotel for lunch.

The street was barely wide enough for a car, much less two women walking side by side in the street. Rose and I were deep in conversation, neither of us aware of the taxi that was bearing down on us until I heard someone scream, "Oh my God! He's going to hit her!"

The next second, I felt my body being thrust against the wall of the building, cushioned by a pair of arms. Whoever it was, had pulled me out of the path of the taxi and saved my life.

"You almost got killed!" Jack said, in a frightened voice, his arms still around me. "You're lucky Pete and I were walking behind you."

I had not noticed they were behind us.

I was still shaking but his presence had a calming effect on me and I made no attempt to free myself.

"Are you all right?" he asked, dropping his arms to his side.

It had been a long time since I felt the arms of a man around me. *I'd almost forgotten how good it felt.*

And for whatever the reason, that warm, caring feeling stayed with me the rest of the day.

Remembering that incident made me smile.

I put my plate on the table opposite Rose, turned my coffee cup right side up, greeted her with a friendly, "Good morning," and sat down.

She had a quizzical look on her face, when she asked, "So, what's up with Jack? He seems to be in a jovial mood this morning, and so do *you*, all smiles." She sipped her coffee slowly, looking at me over the top of her cup, as though waiting for an answer.

"Nothing's up, he's just being his usual charming self." I ignored her reference to my smile. . . ."See Pete anywhere?"

I asked.

"Huh uh."

We were to visit the ancient Dominican church of Santa Maria Novella that morning and I promised to get some good pictures of the interior for my friend, a Dominican priest. Several times on this tour I had been so intrigued with the magnificence of where we were, that I forgot to take pictures. . .couldn't do that today.

The cathedral was exceptionally impressive and I was so totally immersed in its beauty that again, I almost forgot about the pictures. As soon as I remembered, I quickly pulled my new camera out of its case, opened it, and snapped a picture.

The forbidden flash immediately brought a guard hurrying toward us. "Who took that flash?" he said, in perfect English.

Within seconds, Jack was standing beside me.

"She didn't know you had to *turn the flash off,*" he told the irate guard. "I'll take care of it. . .*mi dispiace,*" he apologized, and he reached for my camera, which I willingly gave to him. I had no idea how to turn the flash off.

I watched as he clicked something on the device and handed it back to me. "There, you have to disable the flash prior to taking a picture," he instructed me in a kindly, but technical tone of voice. . ."you won't be allowed to use a flash inside *any* of the buildings here in Italy," he told me, "so keep it disabled."

I thanked Jack and told him I was sorry, but I'd never had that problem with my other camera.

The day's schedule ended in time for us to take a well-earned nap, with time for relaxation before getting ready for the evening.

Rose and I spent more time than usual deciding what to wear. . .on again, off again. . .black, brown, navy? "How does this look?" We were old enough to be on Medicare, but you would think we were teen-agers on a first date.

We arrived in the lobby promptly at six. Our 'dates' were waiting for us. Jack looked at me and said, "You look lovely,". . ."*both* of you look lovely. Ready for a nice walk?"

And we headed to our surprise destination. I had become so used to walking that I almost preferred it to a taxi. There was so much to see and I had the distinct pleasure of walking beside someone who knew exactly where to go.

Jack and Pete had found the restaurant the day before, and hoped Rose and I would like it. When we arrived, all we could say was, "Good choice, guys." And it was.

It took a while, but the waiter finally showed up, and all four of us ordered a glass of red wine. "Four of the house Barbera," Jack told the waiter, "No, wait, make that a bottle of Rivetto. . .the 2004?"

While we were waiting, Rose asked Jack to refresh her memory on what he did for a living. "I teach," he said. Then she asked Pete the same question. He, too, gave her a brief, generic answer.

Apparently that was all the information they were going to share with us, even though we all had ties to Georgetown, and were not total strangers. Yet, it seemed that we were, at this point.

The more I listened to Jack and Pete, the more certain I was that their reluctance to divulge more personal information was rooted in humility. Neither had flaunted their accomplishments, nor said much of anything too personal to us in our daily walks when we were together.

It was obvious they were both highly educated, savvy, well traveled, well-mannered, honorable gentlemen.

They were certainly interesting and entertaining.

As the evening moved along, their typical male reluctance to share gave way to more openness. They divulged that even though both had been widowed within the past couple years, neither was in a relationship at the present time.

That should have been obvious, since both were still wearing their wedding bands.

But I recalled the day Pete and I were walking somewhere and he made the comment, "I have difficulty talking to a woman I don't know," he said, ". . .don't know how to start a discussion, I don't know what they are looking for, and am afraid to ask."

A few minutes later he admitted, "I'd really like to go out with a woman, I just don't know the right ones, or where to meet them."

He continued, "Life is rather lonely since my wife died, that's why I keep working and traveling. My girls want me to retire but what will I do by myself when I'm not traveling?"

I remembered telling him that he and I were having a great conversation right then, and that a lot of women are reluctant to start a conversation, as well.

"Try just saying 'hello' for starters," I said.

The dinner conversation switched back to our professions, in a little more detail this time, which validated my earlier observations. Rose had no trouble discussing her extensive accomplishments, while I told them what they already knew. . .that I taught English. Graduated from Georgetown with a master's degree in English.

Curious about their own connection to our Alma Mater, I asked which school they'd each attended. While Pete graduated from the College, he attended graduate school elsewhere.

Jack shook his head, "Didn't go there, I *teach* there."
Well, that's interesting.

"What do you teach?" I asked. *He'd just said he was a teacher, so I shouldn't be surprised, but I hadn't thought of him as a college professor for some reason.*

"Philosophy and literature," he said. "Got my PhD in the midwest and was offered a position at Georgetown twenty years ago.

"Now he heads the philosophy department," Pete elaborated.

I was truly impressed.

When the waiter returned to take our order, Jack and I decided on the rack of lamb, the other two, different items on the menu. The lively conversation continued during dinner in this delightful, actually romantic, corner of Florence.

We ended the evening on a lively topic that left the door open for further discussions.

When it came time to pay the check, Rose and I pulled out our credit cards as we always did, but Jack said, "Not this time ladies. . .we want to pay for your dinners. We invited you." And we let them.

It was too early to turn in, so we agreed to take a short walk around ancient Florence. . .presumably to walk off the rich dessert we had indulged in, but I had a feeling they wanted to spend a little more time with us.

Much laughter ensued as we continued to explore the side streets, admire the locals and continuously evade the traffic that darted from every corner. More than once, Jack put his hand on my shoulder to gently nudge me out of the path of a crazy Italian driver.

The four of us walked and talked for almost an hour when we found ourselves back at the hotel without incident or getting lost. . .Rose and I might have had some trouble if left to our own devices, but it was comforting to be with two well-traveled men.

Until we said good night to them, romance had not even entered my mind.

Pete gave Rose a quick hug, then me, thanking us for a good time. Jack wrapped his long arms around Rose who clung a bit longer than usual, telling him that this was one of the *most special evenings of her trip.*

He then gave me a tight hug, saying, "Had a good time tonight, thanks for coming," he let go and added, "Now you ladies get to bed because we have a busy day tomorrow and must be up early."

Pete said, "Good night, everyone," and went inside. Jack lingered. . . .

Our eyes locked for a moment, and he quietly said, "Good night, I'll see you at breakfast."

I looked back at him and saw someone different. . .or the same someone in a different light.

Rose and I took the elevator up to our rooms. It had been another lovely day.

I lay in bed for a while after turning out my light, mulling over the day, the fun evening, and things in general.

Even if it could not be Jack, I recognized the fact that I was still capable of feeling, and was open to something more than casual conversation where a man is concerned.

"Are you asleep?" Rose asked from across the room.

"No. I'm still awake. What's up?"

"Just thinking about those two guys. Did you know they both go to Mass every morning?" "No, but why wouldn't they," I said, "with a Catholic church within walking distance. We're in Italy!"

She was quiet for a while, then Rose said, in a most knowledgeable tone of voice, "I was talking to Jack the other day and you know, he's really very Catholic." *Whatever very Catholic means*, I thought to myself.

"He's even more Catholic than *I* am," she added. *Whatever that means.*

"So, what are you trying to tell me, Rose?" I asked.

"Well, he said he'd never marry a divorced woman, and probably wouldn't even date one." Some quiet. . .then, "Does he know you're divorced?"

"Not sure, why don't you tell him? Except that it won't make any difference because he's not interested in dating anyone right now, and I'm not someone he'd be interested in, if he *was*."

"What brought this up?" I asked her.

"Well, it's obvious you two have something going. . . ."

I cut her off. "Obvious? What are you talking about, Rose? There's no such *obvious anything* going on. He and I talk. He's a gentleman, he's a caring person. You, on the other hand have had more contact with him than I have. . .and I have no problem with that at all. Besides, both of the guys are still wearing their wedding bands and in my book, that says they are not available."

I sat up in bed and looked over at her, bundled in her robe, night light on so she could read, but her book was upside down. . .she wasn't reading at all. She was upset, thinking, or whatever craziness was going on in her head. . .all mixed up.

I didn't feel like going into it any further. But, I'd be careful in the next few days to be sure I didn't give out any wrong signals.

"Rose, turn out the light and go to sleep." I said. "This is a ludicrous assumption. . .I am not interested in either of them. . .I thought we were just enjoying the company of two delightful guys whom we will never see again once we get back to the States."

Then I added. "You're tired, try and go to sleep."

In a way, I was glad we were going in different directions tomorrow. I needed less observation.

"May I join you?" I looked up to see Jack standing beside my table with his plate of scrambled eggs, prosciutto, and a couple slices of shaved parmesan cheese, all of which had become our *de rigueur* breakfast since we'd arrived in Northern Italy.

"Of course."

He put his plate down and sat down across from me. "Thanks for letting me join you, hate to see a lady eat alone."

This man was definitely old school.

"Are you ready for today?" I asked. "It's going to be a long one."

"I think so, the last time we were here, Ellen wanted to see Vasari's Corridor but it was closed to the public. I was pleased to see it on our schedule. . . ." He had a slight frown on his forehead. . . "Wonder why it's so rarely opened to the public?"

Ellen. That must have been his wife. First time he's mentioned her name. Caught me off guard, so I let it go.

"Wasn't Vasari's Corridor mentioned in Dan Brown's book, *The Da Vinci Code?*" I asked.

"Yes, it was. Actually, the reason Ellen wanted to see it was because she read about it in his book."

"By the way, did you know they're filming his new book, "Inferno" right now, here in Florence?" he said.

"No! Where? Can we watch them?"

"Don't think so. . .that's why the Uffizi is being cordoned off today for a few hours. . .and probably the reason our tour has been changed to a later hour. . .we're visiting the Basilica of San Lorenzo first.

Even with all our conversation, Jack had finished his breakfast, so I started to eat a little faster. "Slow down," he said, we have plenty of time. There's no hurry."

I wanted to know more about Ellen.

"A few minutes ago you said, *the last time we were here.* . .did you and your wife come here often?" I asked.

"Not *often.* But we were in Italy several times. I don't

do it much anymore, but for many years, I lectured at various schools in Europe, as a visiting professor. . . . Usually based ourselves at one of the Jesuit Retreat Houses here in Italy. Then went to other countries from there.

So that's how he knows his way around Italy. I wonder where else he's been.

We finished breakfast in plenty of time to gather our necessities for the day. The group was already assembled in front of the hotel by the time we got outside and ready to follow our tour guide to the Basilica of San Lorenzo.

Walking in small groups. . .we changed our pace accordingly, as we navigated the narrow streets, then across an open piazza, and if lucky, a wide sidewalk.. . .always on the alert for fast moving cars and mopeds.

In less than an hour, we arrived at lovely San Lorenzo.

The interior was very beautiful and I wanted a picture of the altar. *Flash!* Oh no! Not a second time! Why did it flash again? Jack had disabled it the day before and I hadn't touched a thing.

I hope he didn't notice. That would be too embarrassing.

Why was I concerned about what he was thinking anyway?

I'd soon find out. . .because by then, he was standing beside me. "Kate, you didn't disable the flash!" This time he sounded a little annoyed, and I couldn't blame him. "I thought you did it for me yesterday," I said, apologetically.

"But you have to do it *every time* you turn the camera on. . .it's not permanent."

"I'm sorry, I didn't know that. . .it won't happen again."

And it didn't, because the next time I had the camera in my hand, he was standing nearby, reached his arms around me and said, "Now watch, this is what you need to do," then he slowly turned a dial, hit a certain key, then another 'til he heard a 'click'. "There, that's all you have to do."

I think I got it that time. . .should have brought the camera's instructions with me, but as luck would have it, the battery was now dead. . .no need to worry about the errant flash anymore.

I saw Rose across the piazza talking to the same couple she had connected with earlier. When she saw me, she waved that 'wait for me' wave and came running over.

I knew a battery of questions awaited me. Wish I had more to share with her than the name of Jack's late wife, Ellen.

Ellen, whom I wanted to know more about, would one day eclipse my thinking as she became an unsettling presence in my life.

But I had no way of knowing that, so I continued to latch on to whatever he said about her each time he brought her up.

The last few days of the tour passed rapidly as we crammed what we could into each day. As the tour was ending, so too was our new friendship. Jack and Pete had added a special depth to our tour of Italy, and I would miss them.

The next evening was the final dinner in yet another sumptuous restaurant. That evening would be the last of our little ritual, and I must admit, I felt a bit sad. You can get used to someone when you see him all day, every day, for two weeks. . .and I was getting used to these two guys. Rose was bemoaning the fact that neither of them had mentioned getting together once back in the States.

Our final night at the hotel was a mixture of sentiment, fatigue and sadness as everyone said their good-byes. Some were leaving that night, going on to other countries, some at the crack of dawn, and some of us after a quick breakfast in the morning.

I said good-bye and hugged my favorite people, then went over to Jack who was just standing there, to say good-bye to him.

"I'm not going anywhere tonight," he said. "I'll say good-bye to you in the morning. There's still breakfast."

CHAPTER EIGHT

Back in Virginia

ALTHOUGH I'D BEEN BACK in Virginia for two weeks, I was still mentally in Italy. I gave myself a few days to unwind and settle in before resuming my class schedule, church volunteer duties, and basic routine, but I wasn't ready to let go of the trip.

While I thought I was functioning, I found I was easily distracted by thoughts of a recent happy time.

I am crossing a street in Milan and he is there on the other side; I am on the bus headed up the mountain to Reggio Emilia and I see him at the back of the bus; I am watching the couple make cheese in Parma, and he is standing beside me; I am in the Uffizi, overwhelmed by the beauty within its walls; he is standing behind me taking pictures.

I am in Verdi's home, trying to quietly dislodge the huge cat that is sitting on my feet while the docent is speaking, and he moves closer to me. "If you just stand still, he whispers in my ear," the cat won't bother you."

I am looking up at the Duoma, with awe, and he tells me its history.

I am navigating a narrow sidewalk, again with Rose beside me, and he is walking behind us. I am sitting next to him in a small trattoria, and later, at a table in the covered Mall.

I wondered why I was thinking of him so much. . .was it because he always seemed to be nearby. . .others were too, and I didn't think of them in the same way.

I missed Italy, certainly, but did I miss *him,* or did I miss being *with* someone? A good question.

I forced myself back into reality: into concentrating on my duties here at home, and putting Italy to bed for the time being.

I began by checking the voluminous amount of email waiting for a response or deletion. . . when an email from Rose caught my eye.

Kate,

I meant to write earlier, but I'm having a difficult time adjusting to being back. UGH! But what a great trip! So glad we went. . .will send more pictures when I have time to go thru my videos.

Got the pics Jack promised to send us. . . . Florence at sunset!!! Beautiful! Beautiful! Talk later, way behind.

Hugs, Rose

Same old Rose, always in a hurry, always behind. He sent her pictures? Wonder when she got them. . .I didn't get any. . .maybe he forgot, or assumed Rose would forward them to me.

With a pang of jealousy and feeling petty, I deleted her email.

Where did this new emotion come from? I'm not the

jealous type. And I was never envious of anyone else's good fortune. It's wrong. If Rose and Jack are meant for each other, I should be happy.

I turned the computer off. A cup of tea on the porch seemed to be more in order than what I was attempting to accomplish.

The screened porch was one of the selling points of the house and had been a haven of peace whenever I needed calm or enlightenment. And right then, I needed both.

The beauty of nature, so conducive to quieting the mind, surrounded me. The azaleas were in bloom, green leaves now covered the bare branches of the shade trees, and soon the purple rhododendrons that some thoughtful soul had planted eons ago would add to the beauty.

I put my cup on the wicker table next to the loveseat and lowered myself into the deep cushions. It felt good to put my feet up on the ottoman and sip the calming chamomile. Soon, the momentary quieting of the mind and the body would bring a sense of calm to my disorganized brain.

"Quiet the mind and listen." Such good advice. . .so

hard to follow. Something was going on in my head and I needed to figure it out. Maybe a little self-talk or reflection might help.

After all the losses, do I want to go there again. . .this late in life? Am I willing to get involved in another romantic relationship? And what makes me think there's one waiting for me anyway?

Maybe that's where the spurt of jealousy came from. I felt it once or twice in Italy. . .then quickly dismissed it. But something triggered it.

While I'm not emotionally attached to him, I feel a connection. . .quite different from the "online" men I've met and different even from Nick and Bill.

Despite what was missing, Bill and I had a very close relationship, and I accepted it for what it was as well as what it was not. It was companionship and caring, even love of a sort, but one without jealousy.

Would I dare risk doing it again? It's still better than being alone.

But. . .do I trust myself enough to get involved again?

And. . .do I want a companion or a partner? A friend or a lover? Make up your mind!

Raised before women's lib, we were taught to defer to the man in our life. And that's what I did in my first marriage. The second time around, not so, and it didn't sit well with him.

Not doing that again. But can I be any different? Can I learn to ask for what I want? Can I learn to speak up instead of just going along? And if so, can I find a man my age who has evolved with me? Can I change myself into the person I would like to be, or am I stuck with me?

Why was I thinking like this? I'd probably never see Jack again, but his constant presence in my life for those two weeks in Italy forced me to think about the comfort of being with someone again. Not just someone, or *anyone*, but a man who cared and would be there for me, whom I cared about in return.

I still hoped to find love this time. . .and intimacy. No

longer willing to go along with the *status quo* for occasional companionship, I would keep looking.

I want a committed relationship. *One where I matter, as well, with someone who's the whole package.*

It may not be Jack, but he opened the door, and now I must open my heart. . .what I want is worth waiting for.

What is it they say about prayer? Be specific and the universe will hear you.

A few days later another email came through my box.

Kate,

If I remember correctly, you are off on Tuesdays. Care to join me for lunch next Tuesday? 12:30 at Chalet De La Paix, off Old Lee Highway? I think you know where it is. I'll be coming from school and will need to head back for a three o'clock class. Hope you can make it. Let me know.

My best, Jack

Uneasy about calling the phone number he included, I emailed him.

Jack

Delighted to hear from you, would love to join you. Will be there at 12:30. Thanks for the invite. Looking forward to sharing more of Italy.

Take care,

Kate

Jack was already there when I arrived. It was the first time I'd seen him since Italy, and I was happy to see him, *happier than I'd expected.*

"I see you survived the trip," he said, with a broad smile on his face. . .and he gave me a big hug. We walked inside, followed the waiter to a table he had reserved, and were seated. When the waiter came to take our order, Jack looked over at me and said, "Think I'd better skip the wine today, have to teach a class and not a good idea to smell of alcohol, but *you* have one."

"Nope, don't need one either," I answered, "lots to do this afternoon. But I *will* have one later with dinner."

"Then have one for me, too," he said, holding up a water glass. "Cheers!"

We ordered two iced teas and a light lunch. After the waiter left, Jack pulled out a large envelope from his briefcase. "Here," he said, and handed it to me, "I wanted to give these to you in person."

Glancing inside, I could see a mound of photos and took the top one out. It was the sunset over the city of Florence that he and Pete had taken that last night in Italy, before dinner. . .the one he promised to send Rose and me when he got home.

"That is such a beautiful sight!" I said, as I lingered over the photo. "It must have been more beautiful actually seeing it though," I added.

"Everything is more beautiful when you see it with your own eyes," he commented.

I returned his smile. "It really is."

As I took another photo out of the envelope, he slid his chair closer to mine so that we could view them together and share our memories.

Our tea arrived with the lunch and I put the photos back in their envelope. "We can look at them later," I said.

"No, you take them home, they're all yours." I thanked him, and slid the envelope under my purse.

"What a wonderful trip," I said, "it really was special. I hope I can go back some day and see the rest. You were quite fortunate to have been there before," I added.

"I was fortunate to have met you gals," he said, looking into my eyes. *It was like déjà vu. That last night in Italy, he had looked at me the in the same way, when I sensed something different.*

"The two of you added another dimension to the trip," he said. "I enjoyed having someone to look after. Nothing boosts a male ego more than helping a damsel in distress, and you two seemed to frequently be in distress," he added, laughing.

"Ellen always wanted to see Northern Italy and I'm glad I got to see the places she and I planned to visit, but that she never had a chance to."

He was quiet for a few minutes, but then changed the subject. Told me he discovered this quaint little restaurant after his wife died. It was too much trouble to cook, so he ate out most of the time.

As though to justify his choice, he said, "Food here is excellent, service good, and it is small, private, and convenient. I like it."

And I liked it too. In fact, it had been one of my favorite places to eat when I was married to Ed, but I let that slide.

"I used to find cooking to be therapeutic," he continued. He leaned over the table toward me and quietly said, "and when I learn how to do *one thing* well enough, I'll have you over."

"It doesn't have to be perfect, just the fact that you prepared it, would be good enough," I told him.

After a lull in the conversation, Jack mentioned that the University was sponsoring a series of lectures on Ignatian spirituality. "You might be interested in it," he said, "I'll send you the information, if you are. Read through it and let me know if you want to go, and I'll pick up an extra ticket. . .seating is limited and it fills up quickly."

It sounded like a subject I might be interested in.

Our conversation would have continued, but we both realized it was getting late. "Sorry, we don't have more time," he said, "but the classroom beckons, and you probably have some day- off errands to do." He signaled the waiter to bring the check.

Before the waiter arrived, he smiled that neat smile of his and said, "This may not be Florence, but I feel like I'm back there. . .you sitting across the table. . . lunchtime. . .do you realize you and I ate lunch together for ten days?"

No way would I tell him I was thinking the same thing.

"Seems like a lifetime ago, but wasn't it fun?"

"Best trip I ever had."

I scooped up the pictures, tossed my bag over my shoulder and thanked him for the lunch and for the pictures. I would take my time looking at them later.

He paid the waiter, we gathered our things, and left.

Outside, Jack told me that I should really consider the lecture series, said he'd call in a few days to see if I wanted him to grab another ticket for me, and gave me a healthy hug.

"*Ciao*," I said, before turning to leave. . .I heard a quiet
"*ciao*" from him as I walked toward my car. I turned once
to wave good-bye and saw him still standing there, looking
in my direction. He waved back and headed for his own car.

When I got home, I put my errands on hold, and opened
the envelope filled with the photos of Italy. Many were of
structures, paintings, and statues, but the rest were of
places, people, and the group.

I was in most of them, but didn't see Jack in any of
them. . .must be the ones he took. But as I got to the bottom
of the pile, I saw another bunch clipped together. Those
were obviously the ones that Pete had taken.

Jack and I were in all of them. We looked good together.

His email came within days of our lunch, and attached
was the program he told me about: a series of lectures on
Ignation Prayer. Having been taught by the Jesuits, myself,
I was quite familiar with that manner of meditation and
prayer, but never practiced it with any regularity.

At least I didn't think I had. *Maybe I should go*, I

thought. *We can all use a bit of re-awakening now and then. But I just don't want anyone telling me how I should feel. . .or pray.*

From what I'd observed so far, Jack's belief system was fairly structured, and he seemed to be rooted in the rules.

When I think about my overly strict Catholic parents and the cloistered nuns who taught us, my training *may* have been more rigid than his, but as an adult, I felt a strong need to search for the truth and the real meaning of life. I began to question much of what I had been taught, and began to wonder about the authenticity of the strict rules that were so deeply instilled in me.I feel this brought me to a deeper understanding of God and a closer relation to Him.

Where Jack had lived a fairly conventional life of the mind, I had not. In that respect, we viewed life a bit differently.

I hoped our slightly different belief systems would not get in the way of our friendship. . . and why would it. Friends can still be friends, even if they don't always agree on everything.

Before I had time to reply to the email, he called. "Hi, what do you think of the brochure? Interested?"

I *was* interested, but didn't want to sound too excited. "I read it, and it looks like something I should give a try. Go ahead and get the extra ticket," I told him.

"Great," he said, "I know you won't regret it. It's for twelve weeks, one night a week, and they'll fly by."

I really did not want to add anything more to my schedule. It was already pretty full, but something told me to do this. . . maybe this series of lectures and practices were just what I needed. . . . I was not where I wanted to be in life at this time and hopefully the new spirituality would point me in the right direction.

I remembered something a wise abbot had once told me, "Life always points you in the right direction, just pay attention to where you are being led."

Jack's next words brought me back to the present moment.

"I think we should get our heads together and make a plan," he was saying, "I'll pick up the tickets so don't worry about that, we'll just need to iron out some of the logistics."

A plan *for attending? Logistics? Well, okay.*

Wow, is he organized.

"I thought we could meet at that little place where we had lunch last week," he said, "we can go over the details then. If you're free tomorrow, is six okay?

I *was* free, and accepted.

Dinnertime was far more inviting. Busy lunch crowds were gone. The bare tables were replaced with white tablecloths, and a slim vase holding a lone flower stood beside a candle on each table. All of this, further enhanced by soft music.

A rather romantic setting for a business dinner. If he frequented the place that often, he must have known this.

Jack ordered two glasses of good Italian wine, which we leisurely sipped. "Savor the aroma," he would say, "roll it around in your mouth." I remembered that from Italy, and it was fun remembering. . .that, and more.

Conversation flowed easily, just as it had back there

after a long, tiring day. Neither of us made any attempt to create a good impression as this was not a date, it was a dinner meeting. Two friends finalizing arrangements for a series of lectures.

After a few pleasantries, and without any prompting on my part, Jack began to tell me about Ellen. He told me they both grew up a few miles apart in the Midwest. She came from a large family, but he was an only child. They met in college while both were in a relationship with someone else, but ended those relationships soon after meeting. Inseparable, they married right after college. Ellen worked until Jack finished graduate school when they moved east where he began his teaching career.

They purchased a "nice big house" in an older neighborhood in Arlington with plenty of space to raise a family and slowly remodeled it. Ellen planned to continue working until she got pregnant, but after seven years and no baby, they gave up trying. *In vitro* fertilization, it seemed, was not acceptable to them.

Sad at not having children of their own, they decided

to adopt. Several times they were at the point of adoption when something went wrong. The emotional trauma of *almost* having a baby, and then *not*, was too much and they abandoned the idea.

Since Ellen's first love had always been decorating, she decided to return to school and study interior design.

"And then," Jack said, "our prayers were answered, but in a strange way."

One of his brighter students, an only child like himself, would often talk to Jack about life issues, as his relationship with his own father was fragile. As a result, Mike was a frequent visitor to their home and after a while, he told me, "Ellen and I came to look forward to this charming, happy young man's visits."

Two semesters later, Mike's parents were killed in a freak auto accident.

Devastated, alone, and with no immediate family, he turned to Jack and Ellen, who took the young man further into their lives.

"Eventually, we unofficially 'adopted' Mike," he

continued. "He even lived with us for a time. He's the son we never had and we loved him as though he were our own. He graduated with honors, and with our help, went on to graduate school."

"That's where he met Carrie," he continued. "She's a lovely girl. . .and good for Mike, too, he feels anchored with her in his life. We were so happy when they decided to get married. . .right after graduation, just like Ellen and I did."

Jack continued to fill me in on his adopted family. "They had kids right away," he added, "three boys, two years apart, then five years later, their hopeful daughter turned out to be another boy. They call us Pop Pop and Nana." He pulled out their pictures, identifying each one. "You'll get to meet them one day," he said, while taking one long last look before he tucked the precious pictures back into his wallet.

"We spend as much time as we can with those four. . .their biological grandparents live halfway across the country, are getting up in years and don't see them that often. The older three must be in every sport imaginable, and the little one just keeps tagging along, all three years of him."

I could see he had a close bond with these 'adopted' grandchildren.

He shook his head as though chastising her in absentia, "Ellen's worse than I am though, if one of them gets as much as a nosebleed, she's right there, worrying herself to death."

I thought, *all kids should have grandparents. Those four are very lucky. I'll try to remember their names in case he mentions them again.* Growing up, I only had one grandparent and she died when I was seven. My own grandchildren live too far away, so I don't see them as often as I did when they were little, and I really miss them.

He's so lucky to have these kids close.

As Jack continued to speak of their lives together, I could see the sadness and loss reflected in his eyes, but mostly in his voice, whenever he mentioned Ellen's name.

But what I really noticed was that he often spoke about Ellen in the present tense. Unsettling as that was, I was glad that he felt free to share those special times with me. It was also healing for him.

It's really awful, to miss someone that much.

And, I could relate, though my many years without Ed had dulled the pain.

For a moment, Jack was quiet, then let out a sigh. When he recovered from his momentary retreat into the past, he looked up at me and smiled.

I think that was all he could handle at one time, but he had told me what he wanted me to know.

Dinner arrived and we changed the subject to less painful topics, but I was slowly gaining entry into his more serious world, the world behind the smiles and jovial talk that covered up more than he was usually willing to share.

Hopefully, the lectures or whatever we were going to would help draw him away from sadness and into a happier place.

The first lecture went well. . .no turn-off, yet. For over a month, we attended the weekly lectures where we were exposed to the varied practices of Ignatian spirituality. This approach is about finding freedom to become the person we were meant to be; freedom to love and accept love; freedom to make right decisions. And to see God in everything—in our friends, family, relationships, suffering, sex, joy, nature, music, work.

After a while, we began to look forward to our "date night," even though it could hardly be called a date. We now had something more than a fun trip to Italy tying us together, but we were hardly a couple.

We were still just friends. I could tell he was not ready to date, and that was fine with me. I have always had men friends who were 'just friends' and I liked the comfort zone of feeling free to talk to them when I wanted to, or spend time with them without any further expectations.

I believe it's good to have friends of the opposite sex without the hang-ups of a romantic relationship. And it's also safer.

Besides, Jack seemed much too busy for a romantic relationship, even if he had been ready for one. Aside from his structured academic calendar, his schedule was more than full with so many additional responsibilities.

I would soon find out just how full.

And so, I came to feel honored that Jack wanted to spend these evenings with me, albeit at church.

After several months of churchy things, and the occasional quick dinner after, I found that something more than intellect was attracting me to this man.

One evening, leaving Holy Trinity Church, he took my hand as we navigated the steep steps down to the street. My first thought was that he didn't realize he was holding my hand. I was momentarily embarrassed for him, because a few of his students, who were also attending the talks, noticed it, too.

At other times, I would see him looking for me among the group and when he'd spot me, would break into a big smile. "Oh, *there* you are!" he'd say, and we'd walk to our seats together.

Those little touches began to connect us in a more

personal way, making me feel special. And then the spell would be broken as he began relating stories about Ellen.

While it bothered me, I felt proud of him for the way he spoke of her with such love and devotion—quite a contrast to the many men I knew who often spoke negatively, or not at all, of their former spouse or partner.

It was obvious that Jack and Ellen had enjoyed a beautiful life together and only natural that he would want to talk about her. Some think that talking about the deceased keeps their memory alive, and are afraid they might forget unless they do.

I knew from experience, that talking about a deceased loved one helps greatly in the process of grieving, and I wanted to allow him that necessary part of his life.

But each time Jack mentioned Ellen, I had to remind myself that he was still emotionally married to her, and I was at best, an intrusion into his world.

Hopefully, that feeling would pass, and our friendship might help him over the hurdle of grief. Maybe having companionship for the lectures was part of the healing.

After one of our sessions, Jack stopped for a minute, and turned to me. "It's been a long time since you've been a parishioner here," he said. "How about coming back once in a while? You might like the evening Mass on Sunday. . .it's geared to the young, upbeat crowd, but the sermons are great. . .and so is the beautiful choir. . .give it a try. You can always go back to your new church if you don't feel comfortable."

And so, I gave it a try. The evening Mass was everything he said it was, and I slowly attempted to put aside the reasons I had left some years before. Besides, I enjoyed watching the interaction between Jack, his students, and fellow professors.

I remembered why I had stopped attending this beautiful church, which had been part of my life for over twenty-five years. *It was simply too painful.*

This was the church I attended while a student at Georgetown, and later as a married couple. It was where all of our children were baptized. But instead of peace, I found empty sadness and painful memories, so went elsewhere.

Now, however, I realized it was time to face the pain, the loss, the memories, both good and bad and let them all go.

If I didn't, I would be forever immobilized by the past, and I wanted to move on with my life.

And so, I continued to attend the Sunday evening Mass with Jack. While I hoped that my presence was helping him over the hurdle of his loss, I was also becoming aware of how much his presence was helping me unravel my own tangled emotions.

With each encounter I soaked up observations, and as I gained more insight into his world, I also uncovered hidden qualities in this man with hidden depths and qualities that I truly admired.

At the time, I was unaware of the significance of my feelings, but I felt proud when I was with him. Something about him was contagious. I smiled more, laughed more, but most of all, I felt happy when around him.

It was okay if my friends noticed the changes in me, but not okay if those around us at Holy Trinity noticed. So I had to play down my inner feelings when with him in that environment.

For some reason, I had not told Rose about any of this.

Now, she was coming into town for a few days and asked if we could get together while she was here. I decided to host a casual dinner party out on my deck so asked a few friends over.

Half afraid he would refuse, I invited Jack, too. "I'm also inviting Pete," I told him, "that way you'll know at least three other people."

Maybe that would entice him to come. I really wanted him to see my home. After all, friends do visit one another's homes.

The evening was warm, but a light breeze kept things

comfortable as my guests trickled in.

Finally, Rose arrived. . .forty minutes late, as usual. And she looked lovely, as usual. With her tall straight back and deep coloring, she carried her exotic outfit well. On me, those same clothes would have looked like Halloween.

That evening, she seemed a bit more sedate than usual, but when she walked over to Jack, wrapped her arms around him like a lost puppy, and told him how much she appreciated all the trouble he went to, sending her those pictures, I felt it was a bit too much.

I had made everyone their first drink, then showed them where the bar was. My friends were used to helping themselves, which allowed me to enjoy the evening as well. I felt satisfied with my arrangements: Jack, Pete and Rose would truly diversify this group.

During the evening, Pete cornered me to chat for a while and we had a great conversation. I always liked talking to him because he was so interesting, but he didn't seem interested in pursuing it any further, which was fine.

Out of the corner of my eye, I noticed that Rose took advantage of those moments, and why wouldn't she. . .she was Rose. Jack was her target, of course. I watched her from time to time, either sitting next to him, or moving where he went, and often, playfully leaning against his shoulder.

While he was not the instigator of the closeness, he did not move away from her either. Could my first impression of those two be correct after all? They *did* look like a couple.

Out of the blue, this little ditty popped into my head,

Green, green, it's not what it seems.
Put the dagger away.

You think she's trying to steal your man.
Hear what he's trying to say.

He isn't yours, and never will be—
you're wrong to feel this way

He tells everyone you are just good friends, but...
You'll find out the truth some day.

It was time to put the steaks on the grill, so I excused myself and told the gals standing nearby to help themselves and I headed toward the kitchen. "Can we help?" they asked.

My voice was polite, but firm, "No thanks, got it under control. Be back in a few."

This did not stop two of them from trying to follow me in. As I reached the kitchen door, I heard Nora, announce, "*No one* goes into Kate's kitchen without an invitation. She'll ask if she needs help."

I had to smile. Nora had a tendency to be a bit too outspoken, but she was right. I did get flustered when someone was standing around or in my way, or distracting me with chatter when I was trying to concentrate.

I uncovered the steaks that were now at room temperature—and turned to see Jack standing beside me. "Need any help?" he asked. "I may not know how to cook, but I do know how to grill."

I found out later that he had been in the garden when Nora made her comment and had not heard her.

"You *do*?" I answered, with a question. "I'd love for you to grill the steaks for me, but first let me finish this. . . ." and I continued to rub a small amount of sugar onto the steaks to seal in the flavor.

"Here, let me help," he said. After washing his hands at the sink, he saw what I was doing and began to rub the sugar on both sides of the rib eye steaks along with me.

"That's it," he said, finishing the last one.

I put the salted, peppered and sugared steaks on a large wooden platter, and with a smile, handed it to him.

He bowed, took it from me, and as he headed out the door that I was holding open his arm brushed against mine.

"I'd say 'I'm sorry'—but I'm not," he smiled. *That* smile.

This threw me. Now, what was I supposed to think?

Within a few minutes, the delectable scent of grilling meat wafted across the deck, directing everyone's attention to the imminent meal.

For someone who 'barely knew how to cook,' I

discovered he was very adept at grilling.

And he probably *can* cook.

Had I just encountered another side to Jack—the side of him that could be just the smallest bit flirtatious as well as cordial?

CHAPTER NINE

His World

SPRING WAS ALWAYS a favorite time of year when we were students at Georgetown. I recalled old memories of cherry trees in bloom, yellow jonquils trumpeting, and lilacs breaking open, scenting the air sweetly.

The winter winds, flowing down the nearby Potomac River, were gone, the air warmed, and we walked everywhere, enjoying the re-emergence of the spring flowers, redbud trees, and dogwoods. The only minor drawback was the possibility of tripping on the ancient cobblestone streets and sidewalks in the dark after a night out on the town.

So, it was with a little trepidation that I agreed to walk rather than drive, to Martin's Tavern for dinner one evening with Jack.

"Sure you don't mind the little hike?" he had asked.

Of course not.

I was pleasantly surprised as he took my arm before crossing "O" street. "Cobblestones," he said, looking down at me, "they're dangerous."

How nice, I thought, as we walked the several blocks toward the tavern.

It was more than nice. Having him hold my arm felt good.

As we got closer, I noticed that Martin's was fairly crowded with the usual college kids and the regulars, and hoped we could get a table. Fortunately, we only had a short wait. Motioning us to follow him, the waiter stopped at a booth facing the street, away from the noisy college crowd.

I stopped in my tracks. *Not that booth*, I said to myself.

As the memories flooded in I realized that no memory

is ever totally lost, just the emotion that once belonged to it. No matter how deeply we bury it, some insignificant incident can trigger its return.

In fact, I could still hear the words once uttered to me, in that very booth:

"I love you and will until the day I die. But you're Catholic and I'm Jewish, and I cannot marry you. Your father would never approve, and my family would disown me.

So, I've decided to join my father in his pediatric practice back home in Connecticut. I'll be leaving in June. Please try to understand—I didn't want it to end this way."

I realized I was standing just inside the doorway of the tavern, staring awkwardly, not so much across the room as into the past, and Jack was waiting for me. Still the memory persisted.

Jerry, my first love as a young co-ed, had looked away after this announcement, wiping his eyes and leaving me with a gaping hole in my chest.

When he turned to look at me all I could see was sadness. *"We cannot see each other any more."*

Just like that.

"I'm sorry," he'd added, and looked away again.

A knot formed in my throat that day and I could not believe what I was hearing. We had been a couple for two years, and were in love—so I thought. Something must have triggered this. What was it? I was devastated and the tears were unstoppable.

Years later, when I was married to Ed and we were attending a reunion, Jerry and I would run into each other. He told me that those two years were the happiest years of his life, and that my father had ordered him to stop seeing me because of our religious differences. But that day. . .

"Please, don't say anything," he'd asked. *"Just walk out that door, and don't turn around."*

I'd done what he asked, imagining then that I'd never stop crying.

Now, half a century later, I was about to be seated in the same place Jerry and I had so often sat to have a cold beer at the end of our day, laughing and being so happy.

I was struck by something that would have been impossible to imagine back then, but came clear to me as so very true. With time, one *can* look back and still vividly remember something painful, but find it no longer hurts.

"This seat okay?" Jack asked, looking a little puzzled. Then, "Anything wrong?"

"This seat's, fine," I said, attempting a smile, and slid into the booth across from him. "Something just crossed my mind. Nothing to worry about."

I don't recall him ordering the wine, but when he raised his glass, I was finally fully present in the moment. "To life," he said, with that beautiful smile of his, and we clinked our glasses.

During the meal, and in a rather casual tone, Jack let me know he would be going back to Italy the following month. "Probably be gone about three weeks, for work, this time," he said.

"I guess that's good news," I said in reply to this unexpected revelation. In reality, I felt differently. He was only going to be gone a few weeks. So why was I distressed? We were only friends and I had a busy life without him. Why should his short absence unsettle me?

"They decided it was time to start up the seminars again," he was saying, "so they scheduled me for two this year. It'll be strange going without Ellen, though," he added.

I almost felt sorry for him, but in reality, I felt sorry for myself.

Truthfully, I could see where this might be painful for him. . .but he didn't seem too unhappy when he was in Italy with our small group.

Then he said, "I'd like to have a little get together before I leave. I've asked a few of my colleagues and a couple friends over next weekend. And I'd like you to come, too."

Fortunately, I'd had the pleasure of meeting some of his fellow professors over the past few months, and they seemed like a good bunch. I still felt a bit out of their league, but I couldn't be rude and decline the invitation.

When I mentioned that I'd probably feel a little uncomfortable around all the academics, Jack just laughed.

"You? Uncomfortable around a bunch of teachers? They credit you with helping me come back to life. You can't imagine what it was like when I lost Ellen. I felt as though my own life was over, as well. I felt dead. And so I kept myself busy to displace the awful loneliness."

"And then you came along," he started. "You kept me busy, and gave me something else to think about. I was forced to prevent you from being arrested for taking forbidden flash pictures, and then had to save you from being run over by a taxi or two."

He was making light of our relationship, but I sensed there was more to what he was saying. In fact, he was saying what I'd hoped to hear: that I was not just a casual acquaintance, but that perhaps I meant something more to him.

We laughed at our silliness and I realized that he and I laughed a lot. It was a good, healthy feeling.

Now, however, just as I was beginning to feel comfortable around him he was going away. What if by the time he returned, he changed his mind about me? What if, with the benefit of distance, he decided to start dating other women?

It was unsteadying—hearing that on one hand he wanted me to be with him and his associates and friends, and on the other hand he was going away. After all, to this point he'd only referred to me as his "good friend." I'd once heard him say that he was not ready for commitment, and probably never would be. But that didn't mean he wouldn't date someone.

Sitting there, I wondered if it would bother me if he began to date other women. Somehow, our closeness these past few months had given me a delusional sense of ownership. *What was I thinking!*

He'd already told me he was not interested in commitment, and since *I was* why did I care if he decided to date other women? We could still be good friends.

So, Kate, I asked myself, *why don't you move on and look for what you really want? This one's not moving out of his comfort zone. . .he's too attached to it.*

And still another feeling pulled at me—the hope that things would be different by the time he returned. Our twelve weeks of seminars were over, so there would be no more weekly "church dates" and dinners after. Jack seemed a lot more relaxed these days, too, and less sad than before. Maybe things *were* changing for the better.

I thought, *maybe he's almost out of the woods. . .not quite, but almost.*

I wished I hadn't agreed to sit in this booth. . .the one where I'd been sitting when Jerry had made his fateful announcement. Because it left me feeling like I wanted to trust that Jack would return and still be interested in me—but warning myself not to trust completely that he would.

We walked back to our cars and Jack drove off first. I waited until he was out of sight, then I walked alone down the old, tree-covered sidewalks of Georgetown, trying to take in the sweet scents of summer. . .and let go of the new sense of apprehension.

A few days before the get-together, Jack called. "Kate, could you come by a little earlier on Friday? Say about five o'clock? I'd like you to do something for me and see if I forgot anything. You know, see if everything looks right. . .I'm not too adept at doing this alone. Ellen always did everything. Besides, I want to show you something I forgot the last time you were here.

I agreed to be there earlier, and, "Yes, I remember how to find your place. Sharp right on 26th then left at the top of the hill, house at the end of the wooded *cul de sac.*"

The day of the party, Jack met me at the door, and ushered me into the lovely foyer of this old but beautifully appointed home. I noticed a bunch of fresh flowers in a vase on the hall table. "Did you buy these," I asked him, "or are they from your garden?"

"I bought them, but just stuck them in a vase hoping you'd re-arrange them when you got here. I remember seeing beautiful flower arrangements in your home whenever I'm there. Hope you don't mind?" "Of course not." "Thanks, I'll be right back."

And then he took off.

As I was rearranging the flowers, he reappeared, carrying two large, beautifully framed paintings.

"We bought these in Italy," he said, propping one against the wall. "The problem was where to hang them once we got home. It took us forever to find the right place, but we finally found it."

Moving closer to where I was standing, he held the other painting up in front of me. "Recognize this?"

I immediately recalled the afternoon my camera flash had gone off inside the Santa Maria Novella. The painting depicted the façade of the Dominican Church of Santa Maria Novella. "It's lovely! So realistic," I said.

"Thought you'd enjoy seeing it," he answered. "The other is by the same artist—a portrait of someone whose name I can't recall." Then he picked both up and took them back to wherever they'd been hanging.

It felt. . .nice. . .that he wanted to share his treasures with me. Why did I feel a little unsettled by it then?

In the kitchen, I surveyed his preparations. The appetizers were already beautifully arranged on very lovely plates and trays—whatever serving piece suited the item. He had a thoughtful assortment of cheeses, olives, chips, anchovies, and a dip he'd made. Quite nice for someone who was not adept at doing this.

He vanished from the kitchen for just a moment, then, returned balancing two glasses of wine and a shrimp on a toothpick. "Here, try this and see if it tastes all right." Then, he raised his glass. "To a lovely woman and the best friend anyone could have."

"Thank you," I said, smiling, clinking my glass with his, and took a sip.

The guests started to arrive before we had time to finish our wine so I stepped aside and moved into the living room to be out of the way. The room soon filled up with guests, however, and Jack was still in the foyer greeting the others.

I looked around to see if I recognized anyone—and in a moment, walked over to one of his colleagues, Andrew. I assumed they were good old friends by the way Jack talked about him, and I found it surprisingly easy to engage him in conversation, although I really never had the opportunity until that night.

"Lovely home, isn't it?" Andrew said, taking in the cheerful, well appointed room. "First time here?"

"No, I've been here several times, but only briefly. Once with Father Mark after a session at church and once to meet Mike and Carrie, his "adopted" young couple. And another time to meet the grandkids. It was winter and usually dark when we got here so I had not seen the outside until today. This is a beautiful property, and so many trees!"

"Wait until the leaves are all gone, then you'll really see something," Andrew told me. "Come on, let's go out and see what he's done to the garden," and taking me by the elbow, he moved us toward the terrace.

Once again, I was impressed by the solitude of the place, bordered as it was by a dense tree line. The terrace, surrounded on three sides by a curved, stone wall, low enough to sit on, framed gorgeous potted plants. It was spectacular. Andrew still had his hand on my arm as we moved closer to the wall. "Why don't you have a seat here and I'll get us something to eat. It was getting a bit noisy inside, wasn't it?"

I watched him walk to an umbrella table, which Jack had spread with an assortment of tempting appetizers. "Here," he said, handing me full plate. "Jack just loves doing this sort of thing. You know, getting people together, though he hasn't done it since Ellen passed."

"He does?" *Well, well,* I thought. *If he can make such delicious appetizers, I'll bet he really can cook.*

Andrew didn't seem too interested in his colleagues back in the house so he and I continued to chat. More couples joined us on the terrace but appeared to be more interested in their own conversations, which was fine, as I found this robust, old time, scholarly, gentleman delightful.

His words came across as though Jack and I were more connected than we were, so I responded cautiously. "You've been a great help to him, you know, and he speaks of you frequently."

"Well, he doesn't have much family so who else is there to talk about. I'm just glad I could be there for him."

After a while, I got the impression that Andrew's questions to me were intentionally aimed at finding out more about our relationship. What did I think of Jack's adopted family, he asked.

"He spends every free minute he can with those little guys," he remarked. "Probably trying to make up for their loss of Ellen. . .she was always there for them and they adored her."

I was well aware of Jack's intense need to stay connected to the four boys. He spoke of them quite a lot. In fact, the boys' activities often took precedence over something he and I wanted to do. I almost felt as though he feared losing them as well.

"They don't come over here as often, since Ellen passed," he added. "That bothers Jack."

"Women understand this," I told him. "Men don't, because they are more intense and territorial. Men have a hard time relinquishing their role as head of the household, even when all the kids are gone. But a woman knows how much work is involved in running a home and understands her children's need to have time and space to run their own homes. While she misses them, she understands their absence."

Andrew looked at me sideways, "Hmm. . .you seem to know a lot about these things."

Yes, I did.

I was glad to have connected with Jack's long time friend that evening. He was full of wisdom and I found him easy to talk to on a variety of levels. Besides, he seemed to know Jack very well.

I would later find this quite helpful.

But where *was* Jack? He was busy making everyone comfortable, showing guests around the house and refilling drinks. When he occasionally looked our way, he'd smile but not come over.

He was finally able to extricate himself from his talkative friends and join us. He put his arm around my shoulder and stood still until Andrew finished what he was saying.

Then for my benefit, "I'm really sorry to have ignored you but when I saw you were with this old geezer I knew you were safe and well taken care of."

"Humpf! Says you!" Andrew chided him. "We were planning an escape when you showed up. Guess I'll go see what gossip that bunch of mine is spreading," he blurted. And then my new friend sauntered back into the house toward his colleagues—but not before planting a kiss on my forehead.

It was a pleasant evening and I took it all in. . .made observations, met nice people, drank very little wine and was glad I had been included.

The party was winding down and Jack was busy saying good-bye to his guests when Andrew reached the door. I heard him tell Jack, "Got to say good night to Kate, too. Where is she?"

I walked over to him and offered my hand. He took it, kissed it, then squeezed it tight, "Hang in there, kiddo."

Now what did he mean by that?

I planned to stay long enough to help clean up after

everyone had gone, but after Jack put the food away, he said, "Leave everything else. Can you sit down for a few minutes? We haven't had a chance to talk this evening and it's still early. I made coffee but it doesn't look like anyone drank it. Would you like a cup?" I told him I would.

"Regular or decaf?"

"Decaf will be fine."

We sat in the family room off the kitchen where he filled me in on his plans for the upcoming trip and the lectures he would give in Italy the following month.

"I always worry about being away from this place though," he said. "Too much valuable stuff around and the house is isolated. I have an alarm system, but I still worry about it being broken into."

On one of my earlier visits to his house he'd shown me around the main level. I was impressed by the display of valuable items and beautiful furnishings that filled room after room. When I'd commented on them, he'd told me, "Ellen loved collecting the unusual, and often found them useful in her interior design business. But now I have a houseful of things she loved and won't be using. I have no idea what to do with some of them."

"You do have a lovely place," I remarked, sipping my coffee.

"Lovely and lonely. Just seeing you sitting there makes it come alive again. I like seeing you there."

I couldn't help thinking, *Is* it my *presence you like, or the presence of someone,* anyone, *sitting across from you?*

I wanted—no, I *needed* to know this.

We chatted about other things for a time, then I finished my coffee and got up to take my cup over to the kitchen. "It's getting late and I should be going," I said.

"Thank you for coming," he replied. "It means a lot to me."

Jack walked me to my car, but before he opened the door for me, he hesitated for a moment. Then, he did something I hadn't dared to expect.

He leaned in close and kissed me goodnight.

It was a gentle kiss. The kind of kiss a man gives a woman when he isn't sure how she feels about him, or isn't sure how he feels about her.

But it told me a lot about him, and sparked a new feeling of delight in me.

I don't remember how I got home that evening. I had no recollection of the turns I made, or how the garage door suddenly opened by itself, or how the light came on in the house as I walked in. But I knew something was different.

Not sure how to respond, the next day I sent him a poem by a French poet. He was fluent in French, so I did not translate it—though I changed a few words.

A few days later, I received in the mail, a written invitation to the eightieth birthday party of a longtime friend, a retired colleague of my late husband whose wife and I were friends before they married. They lived about an hour away in the beautiful Virginia countryside.

The invitation was addressed to me, *and guest*. Paul and Helen were anxious to meet Jack since I spoke so highly of him, and this festive party would be a great chance for him to meet some of my other friends as well. Since it was only two weeks away, he'd still be in the country. I couldn't wait to let him know about it—hopefully he was free.

When I finally got up the nerve to call him, *I was still reeling after his kiss*, I told him about the party invitation. "It would mean a lot if you could go with me," I said.

"Oh, gee," he answered, "I'm babysitting for Mike and Carrie that night. It's their anniversary and they have tickets to Wolf Trap. . .I'd love to be going with you, but I already promised them, I'm really sorry."

"Can't they get someone else that one night?" I asked, without sounding pushy.

"Well, they know I like to have time alone with the boys so they usually ask *me* to baby sit, and besides, it's probably too late for them to find someone else. Maybe next time."

Twice before, he and I had been invited to another of my friend's homes and both times he'd had 'something else to do.' I let those excuses slide because the invites were on the spur of the moment, but this was two weeks away. Surely, someone else could watch the boys. . .he's doing what *he* wants to do.

One does not need a degree in philosophy to know that repeated hurts or disappointments breed resentment. And resentment jeopardizes a relationship.

While neither of us was consciously aware of it, our newly defined relationship was already heading for rocky ground.

That Sunday, I met him at Holy Trinity for Mass, but didn't mention the party. The following week, I went to it alone.

Mid week he and I met to go over something he received in the mail pertinent to the seminar we had attended. I really think it was an excuse to see me. *Could he be feeling guilty?* I should have been flattered, but was still too hurt by his not going to my friends' to be overly interested, and I think it was obvious.

"I'm sorry about the party," he said, "how was it?"

"Very nice, you would have enjoyed it."

True to form I maintained my civility during the evening rather than let him know how I really felt.

For some time now, whenever I suggested we do something, or go some place, his answer was usually, "Sorry, but I have to go to. . ." or "I have a meeting that night. . ." or "I promised so and so I'd. . ." He never seemed willing to adjust his schedule.

I could not continue to live with these hurt feelings. They had become a pattern, and were taking their toll.

Maybe I really wasn't that important to him, after all.

A few days after our little meeting over 'nothing,' I began to feel agitated as certain words kept repeating themselves mentally, over and over. They buzzed inside my head like a bee that was searching for something.

You must let him know how you feel, you must let him know how you feel. He doesn't know. You must tell him. He would never want to hurt you.

But he *was* hurting me, and the voice was right, he *was* probably clueless.

My usual pattern of dealing with a hurt was to allow it to simmer on the back burner, hoping it would resolve itself. . .and often it would. But the issue at hand was not trivial in my mind. If left unresolved, I was ready to walk away from a potentially viable relationship.

I slept on those words, but in the morning, they were still buzzing around in my head. Trying to shake them, I slathered some peanut butter on a slice of bread, dropped a dollop of marmalade on the other slice and poured hot water over my green tea bag. I wrapped the sandwich in a baggie and tossed it, along with an apple, in my lunch bag. I would drink the tea on the way to class.

I didn't have time to talk to him now, and tomorrow I'd be out of town. In two weeks, he'd be out of the country. The issue was timely, and bringing it up later would be ineffective.

As luck, or fate, would have it I had a meeting that evening not too far from his neighborhood, so I sent him a brief email that morning before leaving for school.

Jack, I have a short meeting this evening at 7:30 near your home. Could I stop by for a few minutes afterward? There's something I would like to run by

*you. It won't take long. You can call me at school
if okay.*

Kate

My cell phone rang before any of my students arrived. "Of course, you can stop by this evening," he said. "Is anything wrong?" He sounded concerned but I didn't want to alert him to why I wanted to talk to him. "No, I just want to run something by you. . .before you leave."

"Will you have had dinner?" he asked. "I can have something ready to eat when you get here," he offered.

"Don't worry about that, please," I told him. "I really won't be staying long, I know you have a lot to do before the trip. I'll only be staying a few minutes, that's all."

"Then, will you call me when you leave the meeting?"

I agreed to.

It was a short meeting and I called him as I was leaving. He was waiting for me at his front door. Probably heard me pull into the driveway.

"Hi," he said, as he hugged me before taking my arm and leading me inside.

The place looked like Christmas!

Lit candles on the entrance hall table, in the powder room as we passed it, on the kitchen counter, on the mantle, and on the breakfast room table, which was set for two with a tablecloth and napkins. Two glasses of wine were already poured, and appetizers were on each plate. As though he was attempting to diffuse something unpleasant.

"Is something wrong?" he asked, for the second time. He tried to be calm, but his demeanor gave him away.

I shook my head *no,* "I just wanted to stop by for a few minutes since I was in the neighborhood. But I never expected this reception. You went to a lot of trouble. It looks beautiful. I love candles."

I just couldn't tell him now. Not after all this. . .he had gone to so much trouble and I was overwhelmed by his sense of caring. No, I could not tell him what I wanted to at that moment.

"I knew you didn't have time to eat anything," he said,

"just a simple bite to take the edge off."

"This is beyond simple," I answered, "but I really am a little hungry and it looks delicious. Thank you for doing this, Jack, I only intended to stop by for a few minutes, and never expected. . ." my voice dropped, ". . .well, it's so nice."

His caring actions and the quieting atmosphere suddenly disarmed me. I just couldn't say anything that might hurt him now.

He pulled my chair out, and I sat down. After lifting our glasses to a simple "Cheers," we took a sip. I didn't have the heart to undo his thoughtfulness. Instead, I allowed the conversation to embrace a variety of pleasant subjects, gratefully ate the food he had prepared. . .anything to relieve his anxiety. . .and slowly, I saw the weight of the world slip off his shoulders.

I felt that Jack was smart enough to know there was a reason for my visit beyond "just stopping by." And while I had temporarily dismissed his concern, I could see that he still was not convinced.

"How about coffee?" he asked, after we finished the

snack.

"Decaf?"

"I have both." He got up to pour us a cup.

"Let's take it into the other room," he said.

I followed him, and he motioned me to sit beside him on the sofa in the family room. I put my cup on the coffee table, beside his, and sat down on the sofa.

Before he had a chance to say anything, I spoke up. "Jack, I really did have a reason for stopping by this evening, and I really planned to stay for only a few minutes. Then, when I saw the trouble you went to and how inviting everything looked, I couldn't bear to spoil it at the table, but we have to talk."

"About us?"

"About us." I cleared my throat, and plunged in.

"I know you don't mean to be doing it, and probably have no idea that I'm hurt by it, but you're rarely available if I ask you to do something, or go someplace with me. There never seems to be time for us to do things together unless it is church related."

His face was blank. What was he thinking?

I rushed on. "I enjoy your company and I love being with you and around you. I respect you, and I trust you. You're a wonderful person, and I'm proud to be seen with you."

"But I don't feel you have time for a relationship, at least not one with *me*, and yet this is more than simple friendship."

If there's no time for me in his busy life, how can there really be time for me in his heart?

Before he could answer, I added, "Jack, I can't keep doing this. I simply cannot be in another relationship where I feel I don't matter. . .not again."

He looked distraught—as if he couldn't believe what he was hearing.

"There *is* time in my life for you!" he said emphatically. "I *do* make time for you. Please, don't feel you're not important."

I could tell he believed that, but so far his actions had proved otherwise. In my thinking, he could alter his schedule, at least once in a while. I noticed that he made time for anything *he* wanted to do. As a single man, of course, he had every right to. . .but if he wanted me in his life, he had to make room for me, too.

At least it's out, I thought, sipping my coffee. He would now have time to digest this while in Italy. I had let him know how I felt. The rest was up to him.

We had been sitting apart on the sofa, but he moved closer to me and took my hands in his.

"Kate, I want you to know there *is* room in my life for you. I'm just overwhelmed right now and don't know which direction to go. I know I am over-programmed, please be patient."

I wondered if I was overreacting. No. It takes two to make a relationship. And I was a part of his life, but a little too small a part of it, according to the signals he was sending. Part of me knew that I wanted this man in my life, the other part knew that I had to matter to him—or I would have to leave.

"Thank you for listening," I said quietly, "but I keep getting mixed messages, or, at least, I *see* them as mixed messages."

He had been holding my hands in his, but he let them go and put his arms around me, instead. "I would never do anything to hurt you," he whispered in my ear. "Never."

And then he kissed for the second time.

A couple of days before he was to leave, Jack called and suggested we meet for a glass of wine and a Margarita pizza. I wondered if he wanted to meet because of the kiss or if he was just being polite—like, "I'm leaving and wanted to say good-bye."

I met him, of course.

We rendezvoused at our favorite cozy little restaurant in Arlington on my way home.

I didn't want to bring up the subject of our 'talk' the other evening at his house, so tucked those thoughts away because I wanted this to be a pleasant evening.

Jack seemed to be glad to see me, as I was, him.

We jumped right into conversation, had no difficulty finding things to talk about. He never mentioned the kiss or the poem, but told me, "You made me think, Kate."

"Yes?"

"Well, I'm thinking about what you said the other night."

I waited.

He offered no further comment.

We had a pleasant, comfortable visit, enjoyed a couple slices of pizza and glasses of wine.

The parking lot was dark when we walked out of the small restaurant, and he took my arm. As we reached my car he said, "Behave yourself while I'm gone, and watch out for the taxis," he joked. "And if you'd purchase a real phone, I might be able to contact you while I'm away."

He was referring to my "antique" flip phone. Would he call me from Italy even if I had a "real" phone? I wondered.

"Have a safe trip," I said, as I reached for my car door handle. But this time he took my hand, moved it away from the car, and put it around his shoulders. After giving me a tight hug, he bent down and kissed me...and then he kissed me again.

"I liked the poem," he said, "even though you changed some words."

"Yes, I did." I smiled back at him. "Good catch."

"I'm taking it with me to Italy."

He helped me into my car and closed the door. "*Ciao*," he said smiling.

As we both drove away, I knew I had some very tall thinking to do.

It was a kiss, Kate. Not a promise, a kiss.

Driving home, I turned off the radio and recited out loud, in English, the poem I had given him, penned by Jacques Prevert, France's favorite poet.

PARC MONTSAURIS

Des milliers et des milliers d'années
Thousands and thousands of years

Ne sauraient suffire
Would not be sufficient

Pour dire
To tell

La petite seconde d'éternité
The small second of eternity

Où tu m'as embrassé
When you kissed me

Où je t'ai embrassée
When I kissed you

Un moment dans la lumière de l'hiver
One moment in the light of winter

Au Parc Montsauris a Paris
In a place in Virginia.

A Paris—sur la terre
In Virginia—on the earth

La terre qui est un astre
The earth, which is a star.

CHAPTER TEN

Issues

WITH TIME TO RECONNECT with the friends I'd neglected the past few months, I found they had been concerned not only about my absence, but also what I might be getting myself into.

I had not seen Nora—who I had usually talked to every week— since my barbeque, and I felt a bit guilty. So I invited her over for coffee one morning. She had always been a good sounding board and had probably saved me hundreds of psychiatric dollars over the years just by listening and being a good friend.

"So, what's happening with this Jack guy?" she asked. "I can't reach you. You don't return your phone calls, and then you are either teaching or with him. What gives?"

When I explained about the church activities, she brushed them aside and began asking questions relating to the relationship.

"Do you see the red flags?" she asked. "What about the grandkids? You're telling me they always have a game, or some other function whenever you have tickets to the Kennedy Center, or an invitation to some place *you* want him to go to with you to do things *you* want to do. How do you deal with his busy schedule? People *make time* for those who are *important* to them, Kate."

"And the ghost, doesn't it bother you when he talks about her all the time? You're telling me he sometimes refers to her in the *present tense*? That means she's still *there* with him in his heart. Where do you fit in?"

"And," she went on, not letting me get a word in, "you're telling me he's still wearing his wedding band?"

"Well, yes," I inserted.

"So he *kissed* you!—so what? Married men sometimes kiss other women. And so do widowers who can't really make room in their lives for someone new *or* move on."

That was enough.

Nora was coming at me from all angles. Didn't she know I was dealing with the same issues myself? Sometimes, I realized—too late—I did *not* welcome her feedback.

"Yes, I do see these things, but something is pulling me in this direction. I'm not ignoring the flags. I'm just waiting."

She stopped her tirade then and stared at me. I knew the look she was giving me only too well. It said,

"Well, we'll see who's right. Won't we?"

I guess we will, I thought.

Meantime, in Jack's absence, I decided to reorganize my daily schedule. For the past few months—actually, since I'd returned from my own trip to Italy—I had allowed my free time to be completely dominated by this new relationship. So much so that I had even begged off, temporarily, from my duties on a committee at Saint Paul's.

Maybe these next three weeks would allow me to redeem myself, so I returned there for Mass and other services, at least for the time being. But it wasn't long before I realized this pleasant little church lacked the intellectual atmosphere of Holy Trinity and the Jesuit influence that had been so much a part of my adult life.

Besides, the congregation was decades younger, and I felt out of place.

I decided to gradually pull away, and begin attending Holy Trinity—not because of Jack, but because it was now where my spiritual heart felt at home.

And so, now that my free time was "free," at least for a few weeks, I answered my phone calls as they came in, not letting them pile up or go unanswered, as I had been prone to do. . . unless it was one of my children.

One day I actually answered the phone. With an emphasis on every word, my long time friend, Ellie, asked, "Where. . .have. . .you. . .been?"

I bypassed her question, because I was not ready to go into the details of my recent adventure. "So, what's new with you?" I asked her, "How's that happy marriage of yours going?"

She didn't answer right away.

"I moved out," she said, in a much less exuberant tone of voice.

I was shocked. "Moved *out*? When? Why?"

"The house was too small," she answered.

"Too small? Are you crazy! There's room for ten people in that place."

And then she explained: "First, I was reminded that everything in the house had been *hers*. I was afraid to touch anything, and her picture was everywhere. Her clothes were still in the closets, and he played *their* music all the time, telling me once, *That was our song.*"

"And can you believe this?" She charged on. "He talked to her out loud. . .often. I would hear him say, *'I miss you, honey'* and then I'd hear him blow her a kiss.

"I felt like an outsider in what should have been *my*

home, too." Then she added, "This was the clincher. One night he sat up in bed and said, *I see her. She's here in the bed with us. I can feel her.*"

"Dear Lord," I responded. "That's way too much."

"No kidding. That's when I decided to leave. I just told him there was not enough room in this big house for the three of us. The next morning I packed my bags and left."

I fumbled for something more to say.

Ellie had been widowed for some years when she finally met Mr. Wonderful. A recent widower, he was charming and "ready for a relationship," as I recalled her telling me. After a fun- filled courtship, they'd married and I'd attended their wedding. She'd looked so happy! They'd chosen to live in his house as it was twice the size of hers, and in a more upscale neighborhood. I recall how excited she was the day she let me in on their big secret. "We're going to travel the world, she whispered—that's what he promised, after we get settled."

I felt incredibly sad for her.Ellie and I had known

each other since our kids were in grade school, and we had remained friends ever since. When her first husband died, she'd moved to nearby Richmond to be closer to their daughter who was attending University of Richmond. Plus, she had a married sister living within blocks of UR. Even though she now lived at a distance, we kept in touch over the years. Always a fun person, I couldn't have been happier for her at the time.

The truth be known, I had even envied her.

"And what happened to the travel plans?" I asked. "Did you ever go anywhere?"

"We planned them, but he never bought the tickets. And if I'd ask about the trip, he'd always put me off by saying, *Maybe next year. Too many changes this year.*"

I wanted to climb through the phone and hug her. "Oh, Ellie, I'm *so* sorry," I said.

At the same time I wondered. Hadn't she seen the house—with all the former wife's things and her pictures everywhere—before they married? Why didn't she tell him how it made her feel? I wanted to ask her these things but realized it would be foolish and probably hurtful at this point.

"I know you're going to ask me why I didn't see all this before," she said in a tired voice, "but I thought he'd put some of it away before I moved in."

I'd heard enough to make me want to cry. "So now, what are you going to do?"

"I've filed for divorce. I'm actually happy to be free of it all. I'm really fine, to be quite honest. It was just such a disappointment. I thought we'd be so happy. The saddest part is that *he still doesn't get it!* And I still feel foolish. He was charming and I thought I loved him," and as her voice trailed off, I heard her sigh.

Poor Ellie.

Before we said good-bye, she and I made a date for lunch two weeks after she was scheduled to return from a visit to see her other daughter in California.

I hung up and sat there, remembering something I'd told myself years ago after finding myself single again. Ellie had just reconfirmed it.

I will never live in another woman's home, no matter how much I loved the man. . .because I would forever be surrounded by his memories and her presence.

Tuck that thought away, Kate, I reminded myself now, *and don't forget where you put it.*

I got up and went about my day, Ellie's story replaying in my head.

Now—right now, not a moment later—it was time to take inventory of all the things I had let go while dating / not dating Jack, because I'd thought they weren't as important as the things he wanted to do. Now, not later, I needed to begin the arduous task of putting my own neglected house back in order.

In the coming days, without the pleasant interruptions I'd become used to—and secretly looked forward to—I breezed along and in no time the *to do* list began to shrink. The quiet also encouraged reflection on the other issues surrounding the relationship.

Jack was still wearing his wedding band. I had to

admit that. On the one hand, it gave me a sense of security, enabling us to be friends without the intricacies of a committed relationship, on the other, it also sent a clear message. *He wasn't ready to let go of the past and look to the future.*

At least I had to give myself credit for this much: I'd found a bit of courage to tell him how I felt about something in the relationship that bothered me. A first for me. Maybe I'd never trusted the other men in my life enough, and trust is paramount in a relationship.

Aside from his good qualities, what drew me to this unavailable person was how I felt when I was around him. Happy. Stimulated. Safe.

But, it's the way I feel when I am away from him that causes me concern, I thought. I would miss him, for sure, if he returned from Italy and told me it was over between us. But—was this a good or bad thing? I would not be destroyed.

And then there was the confusion factor about the whole thing. Prone to be influenced by other's observations, along with my own mind playing devil's advocate, I found enough reasons to move on before I got too involved.

And so, the inner battle continued: trying to explain away the obvious negatives, uncertain if this is the person I should be with, or discounting the above and waiting to see where life wants me to go.

Right now, I have two more weeks to stay focused on my own life. Who knows how I will feel when Jack returns. I do know that if I can't fit into his life, and feel that I matter, it's over.

As Nora had said: *We would see, wouldn't we?*

CHAPTER ELEVEN

Wait and See

THE EMAIL FROM JACK was unexpected, but I was surprisingly happy to see it. Guess I didn't need to buy a 'real phone' after all. *Seminar was going well,* he wrote.

> *Large group this time and subject matter being well received. Little time for relaxation so far, as am expected to be available for discussion first few evenings. . .should let up next week and I may have time to get up to Florence. . .revisit some of the places we visited last year on the tour. Right now, kind of lonely here.*
>
> *My best, Jack*

How could he be *lonely* surrounded by a room full of graduate students and the ever present clergy? And. . .was I supposed to read something into that word *lonely*?

I got several generic emails after that one, none of them significantly personal. The fact he was keeping in touch was, in itself, a nice gesture and at least he was thinking of me to some extent, but then, friends do keep in touch when away, so not a big deal.

But to mention being lonely? Maybe he really was. It was apparent he now had some free time on his hands. Wish I did. My days would soon be rather full—as I had agreed to fill in for another teacher who needed hip replacement surgery.

In a way, it was good to have so much to do. . .it kept my thoughts contained, and by the end of the day, I would be too tired to miss anyone.

The weeks seemed to fly by and one day I realized that Jack would be home in a couple days. Would he call to let me know he was back, or would I just run into him at church on Sunday? Aside from that, I wondered how he weathered his first seminar without Ellen. Not sure I really wanted to know.

I had thought of him quite often over the past three weeks, but mostly trying to test my feelings against the facts.

No resolution.

I'd have to wait and see.

The wait ended that Saturday evening.

"Hi," he said, when I answered the phone. "It's Saturday night and I thought you'd be out. . . was going to leave you a message. Glad you're home and I got to talk to you instead of your flip phone guru. How are you?"

"I'm fine, when did you get in?"

"About an hour ago." And he quickly added, "Mike, Carrie and the boys picked me up at Dulles Airport, dropped me off and they just left. Good to hear your voice. Will you be at Mass tomorrow?"

"I will."

"Good, I'll see you there, and if you have no other plans, would you care to join me for dinner after? We'll go somewhere different. . .away from the usual Sunday evening crowd."

Trying to digest that earful, I managed to answer him with "Yes, I'd like that."Then, he added matter-of-factly, "I missed you."

His words took me by surprise and it was a few seconds before I could find the appropriate response. "It was different here without you," I said, "and I'm glad you're back."

"Good to be back. I want to unpack and start sorting some of the literature before bedtime so we'll chat tomorrow. See you then. *Ciao*."

And he hung up.

I could see Jack standing on the sidewalk outside Holy Trinity when I crossed Thirty-fifth Street. As I approached the church, he came toward me and we gave each other a big hug before going up the steps and inside to our usual pew.

Settling in, it felt good sitting beside him again. He picked up the hymnal, opened to the page listed on the post, and held it so I could see it, too.

Occasionally during Mass, as we changed positions from kneeling to standing or sitting, our bodies would lightly brush against each other's, not intentionally, but almost by instinct. I liked the feel of the momentary closeness.

The choir was singing the last stanza of "Crown Him With Many Crowns" as Jack and I made our way out the back door of the church, greeted the pastor, then hurried down the steps to the sidewalk.

Before anyone got his attention and trapped us, he took my hand and hurried me toward his car, opened the door for me and walked around to his side.

Before securing his seat belt, he leaned over and gave me a warm kiss.

Then, with a devilish look on his face, he looked into my eyes, and said, "So, would you like to know where I'm taking you?"

"I would," I answered him with a smile.

He put the car in drive, and headed up MacArthur Boulevard.

"It's a quiet little place near the river," he said. Then glancing my way, he remarked, "Good, you've got a sweater. Might need it," and continued driving.

A little later, he made a left turn onto a side road, drove a mile or so and told me we were almost there. For someone who had "so much to share with me," Jack was unusually quiet that morning. Once or twice he'd reach over and pat my leg, as though comforting a small child, and just smile at me.

Something was on his mind.

Whatever it was, I felt capable of handling it.

He slowed the car down, and made a quick turn into a parking area. "Well, here we are," and turned the ignition off. I loosened my seat belt, and realized I had no idea where I was. I thought I knew this area. I guess I *used* to know it.

The place was truly charming. The outside dining patio had half a dozen tables, all overlooking the river, and was not too crowded yet. A slight breeze blew off the Potomac and the scent of gardenia plants was intoxicating. The atmosphere reminded me of one of the small *trattorias* we'd found in Reggio Emilia.

Comfortably seated, and with a glass of wine in our hands, we clinked our glasses.

"To life," he said, and leaned back in his chair. . .just as I'd often seen him do when he was contemplating a thought, or before making a statement.

I waited for him to say something, and when he didn't, I did. "Tell me about your trip."

He looked at me, then glanced over my shoulder toward the river, took a deep breath, and looked back again, at me. His expression told me nothing. And then the words that momentarily caused the earth to fall beneath my feet.

"I never thought I could ever fall in love again," he was saying, "but I did. I fell in love with a woman in Italy, but only realized it after I returned to Florence."

See how simple he's making it for you, Kate. All that angst for nothing. So why do you feel like the world is swallowing you up in its bowels. You said you were capable of handling whatever. Breathe, Kate, stop holding your breath. . .breathe.

"Kate, are you listening?"

I wasn't. I was trying not to cry. "I was just a bit startled, I guess. Of course you wouldn't have told me this in an email, but it would have been. . .easier. . .and. . .you met her on this trip?"

"Kate, you aren't listening to me! No, I did not meet her on this trip. I met her on another trip. But when I returned to Florence on *this* trip I realized that not only had I fallen in love with her, but that I've been in love with her ever since."

He slid his chair closer to mine, and took my hands in his.

It was then I noticed the wedding band was gone.

So he finally took it off—because he met some new woman.

I tried to pull my hands free of his, but he was holding them too tightly.

Too hurt to say anything myself, I only vaguely heard what he was saying until. . . .

"Do you know how hard it is to take one's wedding band off?" he said, looking directly at me.

Yes, I do know, but all I could do was shake my head up and down, trying not to reveal the hurt inside.

"Kate, I think I fell in love with you that night in Parma when I heard you tell the pompous and bossy Rose to stop wandering in and out of side streets. . .you remember. . .that evening the four of us were taking an after dinner walk. You spoke with such authority. At first, it made me laugh, but then I realized there was more to you than the congenial traveler. I loved it."

"Then, once we were home. . .all those days and evenings we spent doing things together. . .watching you, working alongside you, your being there for me. . . . I don't know when it happened exactly, I just know the minute I set foot in Florence it all came back to me, and I knew I was in love with you." He paused. "I just don't know what we're going to do with it."

And neither did I.

CHAPTER TWELVE

Wake-Up Call

WHILE JACK AND I began to see more of each other, our times together weren't what one would call "romantic" dates. Not at first anyway.

He was unaccustomed to dating, I think, and felt more comfortable being with me in a group setting for social events. Once, he said, "Kate, there's a function at the University next week that requires cocktail attire. Are you interested in going?"

I was never sure if he really wanted me to accompany him or if he'd feel badly if he didn't ask. But I would go with him. . .sometimes enjoying myself, sometimes feeling like the outsider I was.

This outsider feeling came from these facts: Many of our activities centered around one or more of the many groups Jack had been involved in for a long time. Each time he attended one, conversation swirled around events in which I had no part, and even though I tried to be friendly, I felt more left out.

I would like us to create some memories of our own. He could still see his long-time friends but in a different setting. I actually enjoyed the friends I had met, but I didn't belong in the *couple's* groups, and couldn't shake the feeling that he no longer did either.

When my husband died, I decided to let go of the still very active group where I once served as president. That was not who I was anymore. Besides, I felt that by staying, I was locking myself into the past. So, after the initial period of grieving, I chose to move on and integrate myself into different groups where I felt more comfortable. . .allowing me to create space for a new life.

I never regretted letting go of the group because the old friends stayed friends. And the new groups in which I involved myself, opened my eyes to so much more.

But this issue of his continued involvement with couples, but without me, would continue to plague me. Did he really want to move on from the past, which seemed to me necessary? I had to remind myself that love *can* exist in such indecision, but can it survive, or *thrive?*

Not without resolution, my soul said.

Maybe my shadow self, that hidden part of me I did not like, was being exposed. Giving a sign I needed to deal with it? It was obvious he had no intention of giving up these groups, so I would have to address the reasons for my "left out" feelings in some other manner.

Over the next few months, Jack and I continued to spend more, and diversified, time together. One morning he called to tell me that he'd finally *perfected* his favorite dish. "I'd like you to taste it," he said. "How about this evening?"

"Perfect," I told him. My leftovers were looking tired,

and besides, I looked forward to visiting his home again.

We had a glass of wine on the terrace, and as we walked around I noticed the leaves were beginning to fall and the nearby Potomac was just barely visible in the distance.

"Soon you'll be able to see the spires of Georgetown," he said, "if you stand right over here." He put his arm around my waist, and led me to the spot.

Something resounded in my head, but I let it go.

"Okay," he said, leading me inside. "Dinner is ready, and we need a refill."

This was no beginner's meal. He knew how to cook!

When I told Nora about it later, all she said was, "That was only *one* dish. And I'll bet he let you help clean up."

Good old Nora. Always ready to tell it like she saw it.

"Well," I let her know, emphatically, "I enjoyed the dinner, and yes, I did offer to help, but *no,* I didn't clean up. He wouldn't let me."

"A star for him," she said.

And I allowed her the last word. I did not care to share the rest of the evening with her.

Over the summer months I had been invited to watch his two "adopted" grandkids play baseball several times, and actually enjoyed the games. Watching those little seven- and eight-year-olds play ball took me back to my own kids' times and I was impressed with how seriously these two took the game.

When the one was catcher, I held my breath as he squatted behind the plate without falling over despite the fact his gear probably weighed more than he did. Both boys were very good, had the game down pat, and I smiled when they tossed their bats just like the pros when leaving the field.

Little by little the issue of the couples' groups I felt left out of became less important to me, and I began to feel a bit more like I was a part of his life.

Until. . .another trip came up. . .with the same couples that he and Ellen had traveled with: a trip on which I was not invited.

It appeared that Jack had rules for our private life and another set for his public image. Rigid in his belief system, he felt his associates would "be mortified" if he brought me along.

Those words made me feel shameful, and I thought, *Well, you can't have it both ways, my dear. I am not a convenience. You can't have your cake and eat it, too.*

I'd been going back and forth in my mind about whether or not things were really working out between us. Now I felt certain again. We needed time apart.

And I needed to have a long, truthful talk with Nora.

Fully expecting another tongue lashing, I found her compassionate. And where I was torn between opposing emotions, she could be objective.

"Nora," I began, "remember when Lia told me I would *not* meet this new man in Italy, but *closer to home*? Maybe Jack really isn't the person in my future after all....because we *did* meet there. And these feelings I keep having about being hurt and left out are telling me that maybe I should...."

"Kate, stop right there," Nora interrupted.

"First, you *didn't* meet Jack in Italy, but *closer to home*.

You met him at the airport here in the States, and when you asked her to describe the person you were meant to meet, she described Jack."

"Well," I countered, trying to rationalize, "sometimes even she gets mixed up. . .sees one thing, interprets it her way, or I find out her timing was off a bit."

"Why don't the two of you sit down and discuss this?" she said. "It's an important issue, and while we own our feelings, they're often distorted because of a lack of right information. Ask him outright, why he doesn't ask you to go. Does he feel uncomfortable inviting you on these trips because maybe he's afraid of what people might say? After all, he has a prestigious position in a Catholic university. Or maybe it's something else. You wouldn't fit in. Who knows? Just ask him."

I wanted no part of Nora's rational thinking. She wanted me to get more information. I wanted confirmation of my own feelings—my observation that he lived by two sets of rules: one for our private life and the other for his public life. In my mind, this was hypocrisy.

At least she did confirm what Lia had seen. And Jack did fit that part of the reading, though I had never told Nora about the other signs Lia gave me. Aside from describing traits of the person I was to meet, Lia had given me two other signs by which I would recognize this new person coming into my life.

So far, I had not seen them.

For now, I was torn between my feelings of love for Jack and the feeling of being loved back under certain conditions, and deep uncertainty that this was *indeed* the man who was supposed to be in my future.

Once before in my life, when I was the most confused and vulnerable, I had found my greatest strength. I would have to find it again.

Right now, I felt I needed to walk away for a while. And—my heart dropped as I thought about it—I needed to tell him that.

CHAPTER THIRTEEN

It's Complicated

BEFORE I HAD TIME to figure out how or where to have this little discussion with Jack, he called.

I listened as he jumped in: he was calling to let me know that a beloved professor and long time friend of both his and Andrew's had passed away.

"The funeral Mass is on Saturday in Dahlgren Chapel, and I'd like you to come to the service with me," Jack insisted, adding, "and maybe we can do something together the rest of the weekend?"

"Of course, I'll go to the funeral. Do you know what time?"

"Not sure. Need to get back to you about that later."

I was glad he didn't pursue the *rest of the weekend.*

Once again, life intervened. I'd suggest that we get coffee after the funeral, and, it would be a perfect place for our little talk. . .on neutral territory.

After that, I thought, *we may not be doing anything this weekend.*

Falling in love at my stage of life, I thought, that evening, *can really be complicated.* Whereas falling in love when you're young means growing with one another and is easier, at our age, both people have set ideas, baggage, and a way of life that may not complement that of the other person. There are definitely different rules.

When he phoned back, Jack sounded warm and loving, which not only tore at my heartstrings but added to my confusion.

"The funeral is at eleven," he said. "I'm glad you're coming with me. I don't want to go to the professor's funeral without you. Besides, half the faculty would ask where you were and I wouldn't have a good answer."

"I doubt they'd notice," I answered.

"Oh yes, they would."

When he offered to pick me up I told him it was too much back tracking and I didn't mind the easy drive on a Saturday morning. He suggested we meet in front of the Healy Building on campus.

"Easy walk over to Dahlgren." Then he paused. "You told me you have a busy week, so I guess I'll have to wait until Saturday to see you." I detected a sigh, and that made me smile.

"Are you sure I can't see you sooner?" he persisted.

I felt an explanation was in order. "Unfortunately, I have several deadlines this week. So far, I've been able to avoid the ladies' lunch meetings regarding the fundraiser. And even though the plans are coming along well, I do need to meet with the various committees."

"I realize you have a lot on the table," he said, "but I sometimes forget about your favorite charity because you don't talk about it."

No, I don't and for good reason.

While I found the ladies' lunch meetings anathema to me, the truth was, I had lost interest in the annual fundraiser for Special Needs. In the past, I had attended the formal dinner-dance minus a date, which was fine at the time, but this year I was Co-Chairman, had someone special in my life, and looked forward to taking Jack as my date.

When I first mentioned this to him, Jack sounded enthusiastic. "You know, we should go dancing some evening," he'd said.

But we never did.

And a month ago, when I reminded him of the upcoming dinner-dance, he asked me to please verify the date again. It turned out it was right in the middle of his annual deep-sea fishing trip. He lived for deep-sea fishing, it seemed. A likely sport for a professor, I might add. And it was one thing he was not about to give up.

Needless to say, my disappointment went deeper than the fish.

No, I didn't talk about the charity or the upcoming dance anymore.

The drive down Canal Road through Georgetown that Saturday morning was quicker than I expected. No accidents, little traffic and I easily found the nearly hidden turn-off to Georgetown University parking.

I pulled into one of many vacant spots and found my way up to Healy on the main campus. While its spires are easily visible from a distance, you have to be in its proximity to appreciate the beauty of the old building and its clock tower.

With time to spare, I wandered around the area, occasionally looking back at the building so as to not miss Jack when he came out.

"Are you lost?" The voice seemed to come out of nowhere—and as I turned, I felt two arms reach around me in a great bear hug.

"Andrew! What a pleasant surprise," I exclaimed. "I'm so happy to see you."

"Happy to see you, too," he said with a big grin. "Been quite a while," he added, "but Jack keeps me up to date with you two. How's life treating you?"

"Okay," I answered.

"Just okay?" He raised his eyebrows.

"Just okay."

We walked along the path away from Healy, but still within eyesight. Andrew took my hand, gave it a squeeze, but continued to look straight ahead. "Want to talk about anything?"

I did.

And little by little, I unburdened myself, keeping the private part private, which wise Andrew probably saw through, anyway, until I felt he had a fairly good picture of my dilemma.

I told Andrew that I did not feel important enough in Jack's life to be considered a partner—maybe he wasn't even looking for one—and that I felt he lived so much by the *rules,* that it was easy to lose sight of our real purpose in life. And moreover, I didn't know where I stood in relation to what he wanted in life, and I needed to know.

It seemed that while I was being integrated into Jack's life, he was not that interested in being integrated into mine, and that did not seem to be a good balance. I also mentioned my disappointment that Jack's trips, including this fishing trip, took precedence over pretty much anything I felt was important in my world.

We stopped walking.

Andrew, still holding my arm, turned and looked at me. "Kate, do you know what the big difference is between men and women?"

"Probably not," I answered.

"Men add women to their life. A woman makes her man the center of her world. Jack is going about his life as he knows it, as he and Ellen lived it. Family, friends, groups, school, church, trips. Everything they did together, he still does. It's the world he knows. And then you came along, the two of you became friends, and he fell in love with you. So he added you to his already full life. That's what men do."

"That doesn't mean it's right!" I blurted out. "I may never *be* the center of his life, but I want to be more than *in* his life. I want to create our own center, where we can branch out to others, including our separate families, friends and church. Is that asking too much?"

"You are very important to Jack," Andrew said in a firm tone, "*and* to his family. They talk about you, even the littlest family member."

"How do you know that?" I asked.

"Because the little guy tells me things about you—but he calls you *Kite,* like 'go fly a kite.' His father, Mike, still reverts to his Irish background and can't pronounce his broad *a's—so* they come out like *i's.* The little boy must hear your name often. Feel flattered."

I smiled. I guessed I should be flattered. At least I felt better having run this by Andrew.

It was almost 10:30 and I suggested we head back to Healy.

"No, Honey, you go back and wait for Jack. He's never

late. I was on my way to the Chapel, as the official greeter, when I bumped into you. They'll forgive a slow pokey old guy for being late. You've got time. See you two later."

And my wonderful friend took off on the Mile path toward Dahlgren, leaving me with something more to think about.

As I approached Healy, I checked my watch against the large clock that gonged every quarter-hour. Years ago, we used to set our own watches by it every day.

It was almost time to meet Jack and since *he is never late,* I wanted to be nearby when he came out. Then, the heavy door opened and Jack waved to me as he came down the large flight of stairs. As I headed over to meet him the large clock on Healy's tower struck the time: 10:30 on the dot.

I noticed Jack checking his watch. He smiled, cocked his head as if to say, *Yep, it's right on time.*

And then something stopped me dead in my tracks. I couldn't believe what I was seeing. Jack, standing away from the building, was silhouetted against the Potomac River, flowing behind Healy. The huge clock striking the time. . . .

Lia's words those many months ago returned.

"They are showing me a river and a very large clock and when you see them together with the man, you will know. You will know he is the man you are to be with for the rest of your life."

I stood there frozen like a pillar, unbelieving. *If Jack is the man, why am I so uncertain and why are there so many unresolved issues?*

As we got closer, Jack looked at me and asked, "Is something wrong?"

I attempted to gather my wits and stared at the river—and then up to the "very large clock," which indeed it was.

"No, I'm fine. Just a cramp in my foot. It's going away, I'm okay now." After we hugged each other, Jack continued to look at me with a quizzical expression.

"Sure you're okay?"

"I'm sure," and gave him a reassuring smile.

I was not ready to share Lia's reading just yet—*if ever.*

The funeral Mass was a blur. I played out my wording and thoughts in my head. Words meant not to hurt Jack, but to let him know what I needed in my life and what I had to do.

Andrew, in so many words, had let me know how men do things. And that I was acting on my feelings, and should give Jack more time. Maybe I needed to reconsider some of my own plans.

After the funeral and reception, Jack and I stayed behind to share a drink with our good friend, Father Mark and of course, Andrew, both of whom were most accepting of our relationship. Only now, Andrew had an inkling of my concerns.

We said good-bye to both of these delightful characters and headed for the parking garage.

I decided not to bring anything up right now, but to just back off for a while, be busy, or *have other plans.*

When the benefit dinner-dance was over and I had

some free time, I could just go away for a bit. No need to discuss the matter of mingling our lives together better with Jack again, since he obviously hadn't heard me the first time. Anyway, I had cover at school and it was a good way to stay busy and see if I could live without him for a few weeks. Maybe forever.

I ached thinking about it, but I was not going to be an add-on to any man's life.

As for the signs Lia had given me—well, they were just that, signs, not indelible truth. If we were meant to be together, things would have to change. Jack's world was important to him and maybe he did not want to change it for me. But my world was important, too.

Luckily, I would not have to make up any tales of being too busy in the next couple weeks as I was overly busy with the final plans for the benefit. And yes, I was still hurt and angry about being left out of yet another event in his life. Sure, it was a guy thing, something he and some buddies had done together for years. But it was still one more part of his life in which I'd never have a place—among all the other places I didn't fit.

His fishing trip was less than two weeks away and Jack called, wanting to take me out to dinner before he left. "Could you possibly find one free evening?" "Yes, I could, but not this week," I told him in a kindly way. "How about the weekend?"

"Good, I'll pick you up at six-thirty next Saturday, then." I knew we would be talking in the meantime.

I had never been to the lovely place he had chosen, and found the décor and service far above average. A small trio was playing in one corner and we had a quiet table nearby.

Jack seemed overly pleasant and happy this evening and I assumed it was due to the anticipation of all the blue-fish he hoped to catch. He ordered two drinks and we chatted about non-essential matters until they arrived.

"Where did you find this place?" I asked. "It's lovely."

"Knew about it for long time, just waited for right time to come here. Glad you like it."

We were half finished with our drinks when he got up

and stood behind my chair. "Come on, let's dance."

"Well, this is a first. What if I can't follow you? It's been a long time since I've danced."

"We'll find out. . ." and he led me to the small dance floor.

Uncertain at first, I found I could have danced with him all night. Back at our table, we clinked our glasses and took a sip.

"You're a good dancer, Kate."

I replied, "You're a very good leader."

When we were seated again, I took another sip of my cocktail and looked at him sitting across from me. *This man is like no other I've known. What is wrong with me? Why would I consider walking away?*

Then I got ahold of myself again. I knew I would have to walk away unless I felt important to him. Otherwise, it would be like the others, and this time, I was not going to settle for less for the sake of sometime companionship.

I redoubled my conviction. I know what I want. . .what I need.

And in that moment, because it was important to me, I told him.

I told him I could not be a sometime, part-time companion. As much as I loved him, and I did, I would not go into the future without the complete oneness that was meant to be.

"We're *already* one, Kate. You know that. I love you."

I looked at him, my eyes filling with tears that I fought back.

"Tell me what I have to do. How can I prove my love for you?"

This was not the place—this lovely restaurant—to have this talk. And now that I'd come clean, I needed to think clearly. What did I want from him exactly?

"When you come back from your fishing trip, we'll talk. Tonight, let's enjoy the evening. It's too lovely to spoil—if I haven't spoiled it already."

"You haven't, Kate. I've known something was bothering you, but I didn't know how to get at it. If you'll just tell me. "

"I need to think, Jack. I promise. We'll talk. You leave in a couple days, and you need time to get ready, and to pack. When you return. . . ."

"I'm not packing, Kate, because I'm not going."

I was stunned.

"I'm not going on the fishing trip this time. I brought you here tonight, because if we're going to a dinner-dance in two weeks, I thought we might need to practice dancing."

CHAPTER FIFTEEN

Something To Think About

"OF COURSE, YOU CAN COME BY," he answered, as though he had nothing better to do. I'd seen Andrew's email the day before, but had not answered it until today. His few words told me he had given a lot of thought to our conversation the day we'd met on campus before the professor's funeral.

When you have a minute, give me a call or stop by my office, the email said, *don't keep things to yourself.*

I'd called him, and was now on my way to spend a few special moments with this wise old friend.

I had so many questions, and felt so unsettled.

Well beyond retirement years, Andrew was still mentally sharp as a tack, and the students continued to flock to him for answers. As a result, the University not only kept him on, but also discouraged him from retiring before he was ready.

"Come in," a cheerful voice answered, when I knocked. I stepped inside the door and stopped short—the room was a mess. I couldn't see Andrew but, somewhere beyond the stacks of books and towers of files, I could hear the teapot whistling. It wasn't just the long trestle table he used as a desk, so stacked that piles of papers slanted at angles, about to slide onto the floor. Books were jammed everywhere, and piles of magazines and journals covered the floor. And yet, there seemed to be within this chaos, an order.

A pair of comfortable easy chairs over by the window could be reached by narrow pathways through the heaps.

"Be right there," Andrew called to me from...somewhere.

And then he appeared out of the narrow door, which I took to be a closet or storage room, carrying a tray holding a bone white English teapot and two china cups.

"Please, sit down," he said, and poured the steaming liquid into the cups.

Then he plunked himself down across from me.

"Cheers!" he offered, as he waved casually to the milk and sugar for me to help myself. We carefully clinked cups.

"I understand that your event did quite well financially," he said, referring to the benefit I had recently co-chaired. "Jack said he had a wonderful time, and would have regretted missing it."

"He did seem to be enjoying himself," I said. "I'm so glad he was able to make it."

"He told me the two of you were going away for a few days. Good idea. You need to leave all the distractions, interruptions, and everyone else behind for a while."

Andrew took a long, slow sip of his tea, but kept his focus on me as though waiting for some kind of response.

"Yes, we *are* going away for a few days," I said, "but I'm not sure how to handle some of the things he and I need to talk about. That's why I stopped by to see you."

"Such as. . .?"

"Andrew," I began, "a woman has a basic need to feel connected, and when she loves a man, she needs to feel connected to *him*. There are times when I don't feel that connection. Maybe I'm not supposed to all the time. Or maybe—this is what I sometimes feel—he doesn't want to be connected. . .at least not in a deeply intimate way, to anyone outside of his family. It's become clear to me that they are first in his life—and that would leave me in second place. Maybe his family is enough for him. I certainly don't want to be there just to fill some lonely hours—or his bed."

I was a bit surprised that I had come out with that last thought.

Andrew did not miss a beat. "Say more."

"He never talks about the future. He acts like the way things are right now between us is it, and seems comfortable with the *status quo,* as long as I'm just around. I'd like to know where I'm going, and if it's with *him.* If this is *it,* I'd like to know that, too."

"Kate, I know what you're saying. You want more than a verbal commitment. But you don't have to be married to be connected. At this stage of life, you don't even have to *be* married."

"Rules aside, Andrew, I grew up in a world of rules, and Jack still lives in a world of rules. Without marriage, will he be able to ever truly share my world and me?"

"I understand his conservative stance on this, Kate. I am more liberal on such matters. But I'd happily have the same talk with him!" he said with a twinkle in his eye.

"Beliefs aside for the moment—look at other important issues. You both have your own homes and they represent so beautifully who you both are. Is it reasonable to expect one or the other of you to toss all that away? It's very difficult to combine two households late in life."

"That's just it, Andrew. We couldn't. I couldn't live in his house, surrounded with all his memories, and he wouldn't want to live in mine. It seems like an impossible situation, not to mention the financial and legal ones."

"There's no reason you and Jack can't figure that out. That's what lawyers are for. But *you don't have to deal with any of those issues right now.* Listen to me—the important issue is your commitment to one another," he said softly.

"Ten priests on the altar, and a dozen notarized documents do not validate a marriage. And it's not the priest or rabbi who *marries* the couple, they simply officiate at the ceremony."

"*The couple marry each other,*" he emphasized.

I hadn't thought of it this way before.

"It's their commitment to each other that creates the sacrament of marriage. You know that."

"Yes, I do, but. . . ."

Up 'til now, Andrew had been sitting on the edge of his chair while talking to me. Before I could finish, he leaned back, slid down, and looked up—as if expecting heavenly confirmation, or searching for the right words.

When he spoke again, the words were gentle, but firm. "Almost every priest here would agree with me, Kate."

Back up to a sitting position, Andrew took a deep breath, and repeated, ". . .*almost every priest here*, Kate. Think about it."

I remained silent. Everything in me said this went against tradition—but then—Several moments passed.

"More tea?" Andrew offered, picking up the teapot.

"Just a touch, please, and then I need to head across the river before rush hour."

"Why not let things go for awhile?" he said. "Enjoy each other right now, and the subject will come up on its own at the right time."

"I'll try, Andrew. You're probably right, it's just that Jack has become so much a part of me. . .we're so much a part of each other. I want our relationship to have some kind of validity. Not just 'here today, maybe gone tomorrow.' I've had that and it leaves you so empty when it's over."

I finished my tea, put the empty cup in the corner sink, gathered my things, and stood by the door.

I couldn't help but smile at how simple he made it all sound. *Get out of the way and life will point you in the right direction.* I wish.

Having aired my concerns, I felt better, and I told him so.

"You offer such great perspective. Thank you for listening."

I wrapped my arms, as far as I could, around his rotund body, gave him a big hug, then headed out of the building. As I walked down the hall, I heard him call after me—"Take care, Toots," and he blew me a kiss.

Toots. I had to laugh. Who used that word anymore?

Apparently as an afterthought, he added, "Guess where you're going's a secret—but have a good time."

Why wasn't Andrew twenty years younger? He was so much less complicated.

CHAPTER SIXTEEN

Into the Future

I LOVE THE ENERGY of each changing season, but without a doubt, autumn is my favorite. Its warm days and cool nights make it easy to let go of the lazy, relaxing days of summer, as it brings with it a new and invigorating energy. In the days following my visit with Andrew, and taking into account his thoughts, I came to my own conclusion. Or started to.

For a few months, Jack and I had rested and played, and now it was time—in my estimation—to buckle down. It was the season to take stock of my own life. . .where I am going. . . what I need and want to do. It was the energy of fall that brought me to my conclusion.

The year is ending—a reminder that we only have so much time.

I wanted to know where our relationship was going.

The small private college where I taught was back in full swing now, and my limited classes this semester were in sync with my busy schedule, which allowed flexibility. In two weeks, Jack and I would be off to *somewhere* neither of us had ever been, for a long weekend. All seemed well enough at the moment.

Then what?

I looked forward to this first trip alone with him, but had no idea what to pack. He had yet to tell me where we are going. The slightest clue would help immensely.

Hopefully, we'd have a chance to discuss plans for the trip tomorrow when we got together.

The phone jolted me back into reality and I noticed the caller ID indicated it was Jack.

"Kate, I'll pick you up a bit earlier tomorrow. The

weather calls for an Indian summer day so let's take advantage of it and do something outdoors. Wear comfortable clothes."

"Okay, will do. By the way, are you still keeping our trip's destination a secret, or haven't you decided where we're going yet?" I teased him.

"No secret, just wanted to firm up a couple places before telling you about them. Where we go will depend on which one you prefer."

In the morning, I dressed in layers; slacks, shirt, sweater, vest, and I had a pair of boots handy just in case he decided to brave the rocks and mud at nearby Great Falls on the Potomac River. His spur-of-the-moment dates were a given, and while I loved them, I liked to be prepared for where I was going.

When Jack arrived to pick me up, I noticed he was not dressed for Great Falls Park, so I left the boots in the house. "You look like a college kid," he said, and kissed me hello.

"Maybe I should I change into something more age-appropriate?" I asked, jokingly.

"Are you kidding? You could put some of those college girls to shame," and he opened the car door for me.

"First, we're going into Old Town Alexandria, to browse the shops, walk along the waterfront. Then we'll have a glass of wine and some oysters in a little place Andrew told me about."

"Sounds great! Speaking of Andrew," I said, "have you seen him lately?" I held my breath. Surely Andrew wouldn't have told Jack about our little private conversation.

"Last time I saw him he was fine. Talked to him couple weeks ago, and told him about my plan to take you away for a few days. He thought that was a splendid idea."

Jack looked at me sideways while driving. "I think Andrew has the hots for you. . .and I know you're quite fond of him. But Honey, he's way too old for you."

"I love the jealous streak in you," I said, and leaned over to kiss him on the cheek.

"And I love you," he said, squeezing my hand.

I thoroughly enjoyed Old Town and the oysters, but more so, our walk together in the sunshine and the fresh fall air coming off the river. Yachts and river cruise vessels were out in force on flat, blue water.

It was early afternoon but we still had sufficient hours of sun and daylight left as we got back into Jack's car.

"So now, where to?" I asked.

"Some quiet place where we can watch the birds, listen to the river, sit in the sun, be alone, talk—and where I can look at you and hold your hand."

"That sounds romantic. And where might that be?"

"You'll see."

Half an hour later, he had driven us to a lovely place high above the Potomac, safely protected by trees and a walled garden. A half dozen bird feeders attracted purple finches and other songbirds. It was truly, a romantic place.

His.

I smiled at his cagey planning.

"There's even food and drink here," he said proudly, winking, as he pulled into his garage.

Once inside the house, it was obvious the whole day had been planned. And probably, I was also sure, our whole upcoming trip. I noticed the table was set for two, along with candles, tablecloth, napkins, and wine goblets in place. I looked at him with surprise and pleasure. He'd gone to some trouble, and I loved that he had done so.

"Dinner is already cooked," he informed me, "and I'll just need to heat it up. Right now, we're going to have a drink out on the terrace."

"I'll meet you there in a minute," I said, "need to refresh my face and tidy up the windblown hair."

Outside, I saw he had already put the delicious looking cheese board he had pulled from the fridge on the serving table, and was busy mixing two martinis.

The warm sun felt good and the gentle breeze reminded me of Italy. I chose my favorite spot and sat down on the low stonewall surrounding the terrace. A moment later, Jack was standing in front of me, martinis in hand.

"To us," we said, in unison, and clinked our glasses—then took a sip.

"To us," he repeated, then sat down beside me.

From where I was sitting, if I looked straight ahead through the almost barren trees at the edge of the property, I could see the spires of my Alma Mater and the river that ran below us.

"Beautiful sight, isn't it?" he said. I had to agree.

We continued to sit on the wall, warmed from the daytime sun, for several minutes before either of us spoke. His arm was around my waist when he turned toward me, breaking the silence.

"Sometimes, it's good to just be quiet," he said, "and feel the closeness."

He was right, and I did.

I realized in this quiet, lovely space—on a sun-drenched fall afternoon—that, as much as the two of us loved to talk, we could be just as comfortable, being quiet. I found this refreshing.

I took another sip of my drink. "Great martini," I said.

"They always taste better when you shake them."

He stood up, took the glass from my hand, and carefully set both glasses on the stonewall.

I could tell he had something to say, because he lowered himself onto a knee. . .and was now at eye level with me.

He took my hands in his. "Kate, I love you," he said softly. . ."and we're old enough to define for ourselves what togetherness means. We don't need our children or the Church, telling us what to do or how to live our lives. Relationships that matter will be there forever when two people are committed to each other."

"I'll always be here for you. I want to go into the future with you. Will you go there with me?"

In that moment, I found myself hesitating.

"Yes, I will," I answered, "but. . . ."

Before I could finish, he added, "I know you're concerned about our two houses, but we can stay in our own places—that's not an issue.

Jack had obviously given this a good bit of thought.

At least I know how he feels and what he wants, I thought. *And I know that when I'm with him, all is well and I don't think of anything else.*

And yet—maybe this was because I'd been so unsure for so long—I did not feel completely settled.

There was the issue of family, and whether or not I'd be second fiddle. The issue of whether I'd really be included in his circle of friends, and whether every time I was with them his late wife's ghost would appear—and for that matter, her presence in all the mementos and pictures in his home was still evident. . .and. . . .

I was beginning to back-track again.

I wished I could know. Silly as it sounded, maybe, I wished there were some kind of sign. Some sign that this is the right path for both of us.

Jack had gotten to his feet, and then helped me up. As we stood facing one another, with his arms around me, a lovely fragrance wafted through the autumn air: the last roses of the season in some nearby garden? I leaned against him, enjoying his strong arms around me in the incredibly romantic setting and moment.

I wanted to share this with him forever—especially when he leaned down and his lips touched mine.

I just wish I really, fully knew for sure if this is the right thing. What on earth was I holding out for?

Maybe our upcoming trip would give me my answer. As if reading my mind, he let his arms go from around me, and lifted my face to his. "Want to know where we're going?" he smiled, titling his head with a questioning glance.

Well, I'd really like to know what to pack," I answered, half smiling.

"Nice, casual, comfortable clothes," he said. "Something warm if it get's chilly and they do suggest dressing for dinner. . .they still do that at the Inn," he added. I think Jack was looking for my reaction because he had a questioning look on his face.

"I like the idea of dressing for dinner," I said. "Women like to get dressed up, at least once in awhile. "We get tired of having our busy days run into an 'evening out for a quick bite' in the same clothes we've been in all day. . .I'm glad the Inn still does that.

I was about to ask him where this Inn was, but he beat me to the next word. "It's getting a little chilly now that the sun's gone," he said, "let's go back inside," and as he took my hand, I felt a warm sensation travel down my spine. Still holding my hand, he led me back inside, turning the oven on as we walked past it.

"Since I've never been there," he said, as we continued walking, "I relied on their brochure which looked good. It's on a private lake surrounded by beautiful grounds and *advertises quality shopping in the quaint town,* so if you get bored with me, you could always go shopping."

That look again.

I just smiled and gave him a big hug.

My concern at the moment was what to take with me, giving little thought to something far more important, something we would both discover later.

The Inn was surprisingly delightful, much nicer than I expected and we found the other guests friendly and pleasant. With ample time to ourselves, we simply enjoyed being away from the distraction of family, friends, students, others, our routines, and our duties at home.

Neither of us brought up our relationship or the future. We simply enjoyed the change of pace and each other's company.

For the first two weeks after our return, we were immediately plunged into a series of standing obligations, leaving little time to replay or discuss our weekend away.

But there was definitely a change in me, and I sensed the same in Jack.

"We *will* get together," he told me over the phone one evening. "Hopefully, things will slow down and we can have some time to ourselves."

I began to doubt that things would ever be any different.

Then, almost as an afterthought, he suggested that I come over to his place *this Friday*.

"Come around five," he said, "it will still be light and I want you to see something." There had been an early snow a few days before and the unseasonably cool weather kept it on the ground. Maybe that's what he wanted me to see. His place covered in snow. I was there last winter but no snow.

The side streets were a bit slippery where the salt trucks missed but his hill was easily passable as I drove up it, only slightly blinded by the low setting sun.

Jack was standing by the front door as I pulled up, but came over and as soon as I turned off the engine, he opened the car door for me, leaned in, and greeted me with a more than gentle kiss, looked down at my feet, still on the car floor, and said, "Good girl! Boots," then helped me out of the car, and closed the door. With the preliminaries now out of the way, he stood facing me with a smile on his face. "Hello," he said, and took my hand, and led me inside.

He handed me a mug of warm cider and said, "Come on, before the sun sets, bring the mug with you, we'll have a martini later," and with his free arm, guided me to the terrace.

I could see footprints in the snow leading from the terrace to the end of the property and back again. He let go of my hand and motioned me to follow him along the same narrow path.

The view was spectacular. The way the sun bounced off Healy Building on Georgetown's campus in the distance and then cast a glistening ray on the Potomac below gave the moment its power.

"Bet you never saw your Alma Mater from this angle, did you? The setting sun and the snow and the spires of Georgetown. Beautiful, isn't it?"

And it was.

"I came out here last evening and knew you had to see this, too. I'm so glad you could get here before the sun set. It's gone in a minute, you know.

And so is life.

I followed Jack back to the stone terrace which was a bit more stable under foot than the snow-covered earth. "Warm enough?" he asked.

"Actually, I'm amazed at how warm the sun still is," I said, and loosened my jacket.

Jack turned around, and, as if to say something, slid his arms inside my open jacket, wrapping them around me.

"You know," he said, "those few days away made me realize how comfortable we are together."

He was reading my mind. Not a good sign. Now, I'd have to pay more attention to my thoughts when in his presence.

"I love you," he whispered, and then, he kissed me.

We stood there for the longest time, close together, locked in that kiss, immersed in our love for one another.

From across the river, the gong of the large clock on Healy began to strike the hour. And the words of Lia, the psychic, rushed into my head.

"They are showing me a large clock and a body of water, looks like a river," she was saying. *"When you see them both together with the man, you will know he is the one you are to be with."*

All those months of doubt, of wondering if this was right for us, if the obstacles could ever be dealt with. . .I mentally tossed them onto the snow, to melt away with it.

Jack drew his face back slightly. "What is it? Something wrong?" he asked. Then brushing a tear from my cheek, he asked again, *"Is something wrong?*

I shook my head no, and leaned into him.

No, my love. Nothing is wrong. Everything is right.

ABOUT THE AUTHOR

After twenty-five years as an office nurse in an OB/GYN practice, Nancy finally retired this past summer. A writer for most of her adult life, she recently published two memoirs.

A MOTHER NEVER FORGETS, is the story of her search for the daughter she relinquished to adoption at birth. The other, A WAY OUT, was written to help those trapped in an abusive relationship. Both are available on Amazon.

A founding member of Great Falls Writer's Group, Nancy continues to enjoy learning and sharing through interaction with other writers and authors.

The mother of six adult children, Nancy was always active in her children's schools and activities. Now, she relishes whatever time they have to share with her.

Her seven grandchildren range in age from twelve to thirty-three, and she will soon become a great-grandmother. Family and home, friends and God are the bedrock of her life.

"Gardening keeps me fit," she says, "but love and having a purpose are what keep me young."

Nancy lives in Great Falls, Virginia.

Made in the USA
Columbia, SC
07 May 2018